HONEYSUCKLE
AND
CUSTARD CREAMS

DEIRDRE FOLEY

For
Helena and Melina

Good Lord, how sweetly smells the honeysuckle
In the hushed night, as if the world were one
Of utter peace, and love, and gentleness!
                                        Tennyson

1978

Prologue

For most of the passengers disembarking the evening flight from London Heathrow to Aldergrove Airport in Belfast, neither the sleet nor the wind can dampen their spirits. For these passengers, there is an urgency in the air, a collective excitement. They scurry across the slippery tarmac and tumble into the baggage reclaim area where they help each other dislodge trolleys from other trolleys. There is banter, animated chit-chat, until the conveyor belt creaks into motion and the first suitcase appears. Finally, a silence of sorts descends as the trolleys troop towards the exit where the mammies and daddies and grannies and grandads are gathered, ready to transport luggage and loved ones to towns and villages spread across the length and breadth of Northern Ireland.

In the ladies' toilet, off the baggage reclaim area, Sinead Reilly is leaning against a cubicle wall and tearing off yet another piece of flimsy toilet roll. She wipes her eyes one last time before putting her glasses back on and flushing the tissue away. Stepping outside the cubicle, she makes for a washbasin. The place is empty, thankfully. Staring into the cracked mirror, she drags some strands of damp hair from her cheeks and tucks them behind her ears. Then lowering her gaze, she grips the sides of the washbasin and focuses her attention for a moment on a tiny blob of dirt nestling close to the plug hole. She swallows hard. Finally, almost in slow motion, she lifts her battered duffel bag. The weight of it snaps her back to reality. She finds composure; her breathing is fine, her vision less blurred. She picks up her step as she heads towards the baggage reclaim area once more. But the tranquillity that hits her when she gets there threatens to send her into panic mode all over again. Where the hell is everyone? Face blazing, she hauls her lone suitcase off the dead conveyor belt, dumps it onto a trolley and races towards the exit.

A middle-aged man of average height has just arrived in the waiting area. He is late. The two-hour drive had been arduous. Delays at the army checkpoints had seemed longer than usual. The shoulders and back of his beige trench coat are drenched. His face is numb. He should have taken a hat and scarf with him. But as he wipes the steam from his glasses with the hem of his coat and scans the warm waiting area, his cheeks are already starting to tingle and the shivers are rapidly subsiding. Where is she? His palms and armpits will start to sweat soon. Rubbing his hands on the sides of his coat, he moves closer to the draughty exit door of the terminal building. There, he presses his back against a column and waits for his daughter to appear.

November
1968

1. SINEAD

'SINEAD, GIVE US that tray and run up to the house quickly.'

Mammy's pretending to be calm.

'There's a tin of biscuits in the linen basket. Bring it down as fast as you can.'

She pushes me into the living room.

'And bring the tin of tea down as well, just to be on the safe side. Go on, get a move on and stop your huffing. You'll still be ten when you blow your candles out.'

'It's not the same, Mammy. I want to blow them out today … and I'm not flamin' huffing.'

'Don't you dare be cheeky like that to me, Sinead. And show a bit of respect. Your father's mother's just died. Stop acting like a baby.'

What the flippin' hell is she talking about? I'm not being flamin' cheeky. Just because I can't see what the big deal is. I hardly even knew Granny Reilly, for Pete's sake. She's been on her deathbed forever. I'm not saying I don't feel a bit sad.

I do. I swear. But why did she have to die right now? I don't want to be serving smelly egg and onion sandwiches and biscuits at my granny's flamin' wake to a crowd of old fogeys and busybodies who are making Mammy's temper worse than it normally is in the morning. And why can't someone else go get the biscuits? It's pishing outside.

'Sinead, pet, could you get Mrs Doyle a cup of tea?' Aunty Eileen says, just as I'm about to ask if she's sitting on my coat.

She's been on the couch for over an hour, sobbing and sniffling like she just got the shock of her life. Sure has she not been praying for years that the Lord would be kind and take Granny up to heaven with him? Crocodile tears, I heard Mammy whisper. And what if I don't want to get Mrs cross-eyed Doyle a cup of stinky tea? That's all Mrs Doyle does – drink tea at wakes and get a feed of sandwiches. It's a full-time occupation according to Mammy.

'Is my coat there, Aunty Eileen? I have to go up to the house for more biscuits.' I can play deaf as good as grown-ups can.

'All the coats are upstairs in the back room where your granda has his fishing gear.'

Thanks for nothing Aunty Eileen.

Right now I'm in no mood to have to pass the wake room again. I feel like boking every time I get near the coffin. It's my first ever wake. I only looked inside once but I wish I hadn't. Granny's corpse gives me the heebie-jeebies with those rosary beads twisted around her fingers like she's ready to say three Hail Marys and a Glory Be any second now. I'm glad I didn't see Mr Robinson in a coffin.

Poor Mr Robinson.

I wonder if his face is ironed out and plastic-looking

too? One thing's for sure – there aren't any creepy rosary beads in his coffin. Protestants don't have rosary beads. If Mr Robinson was still alive I'd sneak up for a visit, even without a bunch of honeysuckle. I wouldn't care one bit if Mammy and Daddy and the rest of them gave out to me. Mr Robinson was my friend, not a stranger, and he wouldn't stop me blowing out candles today.

By the time I get back downstairs with my coat, a whole load of new people are coming up the garden path. Strangers, the lot of them. Except for Nora Diver. Everyone knows Stingy Mingy Nora. Daddy says her shop makes more money in a day than most people earn in a month.

'Sorry for your loss, pet.'

I'm not your flamin' pet, Mrs Diver.

'Thanks, Mrs Diver.'

I have to squeeze past her.

'Are you all right, pet?' she calls after me.

No, I'm not all right, Mrs Diver, if you really want to know.

'Yes, I'm fine, Mrs Diver. Thank you.'

I have to keep a tight lip around the likes of Nora Diver. She's the 'legendary town gossip like her mother was before her'. Aunty Eileen's exact words.

I'm not the greatest at keeping my lip tight. I've got a mouth so big my two feet could fit inside, as Kieran loves telling the whole world. And talking about Kieran, why isn't he down serving sandwiches and biscuits? That's what I'd like to know. He's the eldest, not me.

I'm glad to get away from Eden Drive for a bit, even if it does mean getting soaked. My grandparents' house is the shabbiest in the row, with scabby paint and chipped window frames. It's as miserable inside too, even without a corpse.

Eden Drive must be the oldest council estate in the town. The street's hardly the width of McNally's alleyway. Gardens the size of matchboxes. I'm lucky to be living in Drummore Court. I like having a gigantic green in the middle of the estate.

This coat hood is far too small – my flamin' fringe is already dripping onto my glasses. Plus the piece of cardboard inside my right shoe is squelching. At this rate the hole will be the size of a half-crown come Daddy's payday.

Right, I'm going up the back way. I don't care about the muck. I don't care about anything any more. This is the worst day of my life. But I'm not going to cry. No way. Though it's hard not to with the picture of Mr Robinson's house in my head. Or what used to be Mr Robinson's house.

It's weird how he had been living there for years but I only became his friend in August. I hadn't meant to call out that day. He hadn't even noticed me standing in the back garden as he was walking up the lane.

'Hello, Mr Robinson.'

The words had just popped out. I wasn't expecting him to stop dead in his tracks. He usually never spoke to anyone. Even my friend Linda, who is also a Protestant, couldn't get a peep out of him. Mrs Robinson would always say hello for the both of them, and after she died in March we hardly ever saw Mr Robinson.

'Hello yourself. It's Sinead, isn't it?' he replied in the posh way Protestants have of talking. They say things differently from us Catholics sometimes, like Londonderry instead of Derry or Ulster instead of the North of Ireland.

'How do you know my name, Mr Robinson?' I asked him in my politest voice.

He straightened his shoulders. Mr Robinson had the droopiest shoulders I have ever seen.

'I suppose I know your name much the same way you know my name,' he said.

I hadn't thought of that. Mr Robinson was very clever. Nearly as clever as Daddy.

'And what are you doing there?' he added.

'I'm gathering honeysuckle for my mammy and daddy. It's their wedding anniversary today.'

'Honeysuckle are Mildred's favourite flowers, but we don't have a lovely hedge full of them like you do,' he said, coming right up close to the fence.

My knees went wobbly and I took a step back. I didn't know what to say. Luckily Mr Robinson spoke again.

'And how many years are being celebrated today?'

'What?'

'Your mother and father … how long have they been married?'

'Oh, twelve years. They got married on the eleventh of August 1956.'

'Well, they're very lucky to have such a thoughtful daughter,' he said, not budging an inch.

The only thing in my head was the ghost of Mrs Robinson. So thank God Mr Robinson went back to drooping his shoulders as he said he had to be getting home. I was ready to make a run for it.

'It's ironing day today and the windows could do with a wash. Bye-bye for now, Sinead.'

'Bye-bye, Mr Robinson.'

And off he went.

But it was impossible to get him out of my head.

I tortured Mammy for information, but all she could tell

me was that he used to have a very good job in the Post Office and he'd only just retired when Mrs Robinson passed away.

Daddy didn't say much about him either.

'Mr Robinson is from county Antrim. He's a quiet man who likes to keep himself to himself.'

'Why?'

'That's just the way it is with some people. They prefer being alone.'

'I wouldn't want to be alone. I don't think there is anyone in the world who wants to be lonely.'

'Being alone is not the same as being lonely.'

But that made no sense to me. No sense at all.

All week I kept thinking about Mr Robinson in his house, alone *and* lonely. So in the end I filled a jam jar with water, squeezed as many honeysuckle as I could into it and marched up the back lane to his house.

The gate creaked so loudly I was sure he would hear it and come to the door. He didn't though. Not even after I'd rapped it a couple of times. The windows upstairs and downstairs were shut and the curtains were closed. So I was just bending down to put the honeysuckle safely against the wall beside the steps for Mr Robinson to find later, when the door began to open very, very slowly, just like it does in horror films. The jam jar nearly slipped out of my hand.

'Oh, Mr Robinson, hello! I thought you were out,' I said, standing up like a shot, my heart pounding.

The door was only half open and Mr Robinson was hiding behind it in his pyjamas. No one wears pyjamas at three o'clock in the afternoon. Not unless they're sick.

'I brought you some honeysuckle,' I said, lifting the jam jar up for him to see.

He didn't look sick. He squinted at the flowers and poked his head out a bit further from behind the door but he said nothing. Some greasy white hair was stuck to his forehead and his face wasn't shaved.

'You said they were Mrs Robinson's favourites.'

Still he said nothing. But the second I held out the jar for him to take he recognised me.

'Oh, of course ... yes ... Sinead ... Sinead Reilly from number seven ... honeysuckle ... so beautiful. Thank you very, very much, Sinead ... Mildred's favourite flowers, that's right. How clever of you to remember.' He had no teeth in so his voice sounded different. 'It's so kind of you to bring us flowers. Wait there a wee second,' he said.

He was back in a jiffy holding a thruppenny bit for me to take.

'No, thank you, Mr Robinson,' I said politely, though I was dying to take it.

But when he insisted, it dawned on me that Mr Robinson wasn't exactly a stranger so I thanked him and started heading back towards the gate.

'Come up any time you like,' he called out.

'I will. I'll come again next week if you want.'

That was how we became friends.

But I have to get him out of my head now because the tears are tripping me, I'm shivering with the cold and if I don't get the box of biscuits down to Granny's wake soon Mammy will kill me. I wish I didn't have to go back down again. The fire is on full in our living room and I'd rather stay here with the rest of them. I've a good mind to send Kieran down with the tea and biscuits.

Where is Kieran anyway?

Niamh is splayed like an octopus on the floor playing

tiddlywinks with Eamon – and losing by the looks of things. How is it possible to get beaten by a four-year-old?

Perched on the arm of the couch is baby Michael. Niall is looking after him and being an eejit with his ridiculous impressions of daleks and cybermen.

'Hey, Sinead, what are you doing back up? What's it like – the body, I mean?' Niamh asks.

'Horrible.'

'What do you mean?'

'I'll tell you later.'

'I don't see why only you and Kieran are allowed down. I'm not a baby.'

'Actually, you *are* a baby. A big moany, groany, baby.'

'Shut up, Sinead.'

'Shut up yourself, Niamh!'

Does she honestly think she'd be able to look at a dead body up close? Some chance. Niamh's afraid of her own shadow. She'd pee her pants in a second. There she goes, turning her face away in a huff as if I'm to blame for everything.

Niall has stopped acting the cod and is staring at me. I wipe away the tears. He's a big softy really, even if he can be a twat.

Upstairs the boys' bedroom door is closed, but as soon as I go into Mammy's room I hear Kieran moving around. I've only just heaved the Crawford's biscuit tin out from under the pile of special occasion towels in the linen basket when he appears like a ghost behind me.

'Hey, where are you going with that?' he asks.

'None of your business. Where have you been?' I snap back.

Lazy Sod.

'Here, give us a couple.'

'No! They're for the wake.'

The nerve of him. I have to push past to get onto the landing.

'And why are you not down helping?' I shout.

'Piss off, Sinead,' he shouts back, and slams his bedroom door in my face.

I swear to God I could slap him. He has turned into a monster since he started at the grammar school. Every second word is the F-word. I hate him. And now my flamin' lip is bleeding where I've bitten into it. The taste of blood makes me want to vomit. What about 'Happy Birthday, Sinead'? Wait till *his* birthday comes around. He'll soon see what it feels like.

By the time I get back to the wake there are more visitors than before and Mammy is about to have a fit.

'Jesus, Mary and Joseph, what kept you, Sinead?'

She snatches the tins off me.

'Quickly, go gather up the empty cups and plates. And tell your father I want to speak to him for a minute.'

Tell him yourself.

I'm sick to the stomach of bad tempers. Daddy is upstairs on the landing with Granda and Uncle Brendan. They each have a glass of whiskey in their hands. What is Daddy doing with a glass of whiskey? Uncle Brendan, yes. Granda, yes. But Daddy?

'Daddy, Mammy wants you in the scullery.'

Is he deaf as well as sad?

'Daddy, Mammy says—'

'I heard you. I'll be down in a minute.'

Another bad temper. But at least *he* has an excuse.

The flowered wallpaper running the length of the banister

13

is grubby and the floorboards are showing through the carpet. Disgusting. The house smells too. An old people's smell.

'Here, Sinead, give us those dirty cups,' Geraldine says as I go into the scullery.

Geraldine is the official washer-up. She's terrified of coffins, even though she's sixteen. Geraldine is definitely my favourite cousin … and she's gorgeous-looking. Her face is like a film star's, with lovely swarthy skin and not a freckle in sight, the complete opposite of Aunty Eileen. Most of the Donnellys have swarthy skin. Lucky ducks.

'It's horrible this happening on your birthday, Sinead. I'll bake you an extra large cake when it's all over and you can blow out your candles twice,' she says after taking the empty cups and giving me another big hug, the third so far today. Easy to see why she's my favourite cousin. 'Here, take this plate of biscuits, leave them upstairs and then come straight on down again. You can pretend to be helping me.'

'Thanks Geraldine.'

I think Geraldine is everyone's favourite cousin.

I take the plate from her and I'm pushing my way through the living room again when I catch sight of some custard creams peaking out from under the ginger snaps on the plate. Custard creams – Mr Robinson's favourite biscuits. Him coming in and out of my brain today is making my vomity feeling even worse than it already is.

I miss him. He was like Geraldine, so kind. The second time I visited him was great. The windows were open and the curtains were drawn. I hardly had to knock the door at all before he flung it wide open with a humongous smile, teeth and all. There wasn't even a droop in his shoulders. He was wearing a blue suit and tie and his hair was Brylcreemed like it used to be when Mrs Robinson was alive.

'Hello, Mr Robinson,' I said, handing him the bunch of honeysuckle. 'I didn't have a jam jar to put them in.' I'd wrapped the flowers in a piece of tin foil because Granny Boyle needed all our empty jars for her gooseberry jam.

'Why, Sinead, they're even more v-v-vivacious than the previous bunch,' he said, his cheeks as red as a tomato. 'Let's get them into the v-v-vase, shall we?' he said, and he held the door open for me to go inside.

I could have sworn I hadn't heard him stutter the last time. Or the time before that. I stepped into the back hall and followed him into his scullery, even though I'd no intention of staying. I'd only ever been inside one other Protestant house – Linda's. Her scullery is always clean and tidy but Mr Robinson's was the cleanest, tidiest scullery I'd ever seen, Protestant or Catholic. There were two spotless tea towels hanging neatly on a little rail and there was one of those dish racks on the wall where the plates are all facing out the ways, with tea cups dangling from brass hooks below.

'Your kitchen is lovely and clean,' I said.

'Oh, Mildred is very house-proud, and Mrs Duncan comes in every week to help out. We wouldn't manage without her.'

For some reason him mentioning Mrs Robinson wasn't as weird as before.

He lifted a vase from his window sill with the old bunch of withering honeysuckle still in it.

'Don't let me forget to give you your j-j-jam jar before you leave,' he said, emptying the vase and filling it with clean water. Then he put the new bunch in and carried the vase towards the living room where he put it on top of a piano.

'Can you play the piano, Mr Robinson?'

'Lord no,' he joked. 'Mildred is the musician in this house.

These hands of mine were most definitely not made for anything as c-c-complicated as playing a piano, but Mildred would like to believe otherwise. She's been trying to teach me for years. I think she's finally given up on me though.'

He fiddled about for a bit with the vase.

'There! That's the place for them. Now, young lady, can we offer you some refreshments?'

Mr Robinson's suite of furniture looked brand new. There was no lino on his floor that I could see, only carpet. He pointed to a coffee table where there were two glasses, a jug of orange juice and a plate of custard creams.

'I love custard creams,' I said when he offered me the plate.

'There's another thing we all have in common, then. In fact, I don't mind admitting that I think custard creams are the best biscuits ever made. You can keep all those fancy chocolate ones. There's nothing to beat a custard cream, as Mildred says. Here, sit down. Do you like orange juice? Of course you like orange juice – silly question. But if you'd prefer milk, I've plenty to spare. Or if you want I could make you a cup of tea? Oh dear, I should have bought some lemonade. I never thought. We don't drink lemonade ourselves. Now tea, on the other hand, we could drink until the cows come home.'

He laughed and sat down on the settee and poured himself some juice too. I hadn't the heart to tell him I don't really like orange juice. Then he began telling me about his ruby wedding anniversary and before I knew it a box of photographs was plonked on the table. And he had stopped stuttering.

There were photographs at the beach, photographs in the mountains, photographs at Christmas. He explained who everyone was. I soon figured out that everyone was Mrs Robinson's relatives. Because Mr Robinson was an orphan! No Mammy, Daddy, brothers, sisters, aunts, uncles … nothing. I'd never met an orphan before.

'So you don't have any relatives at all, Mr Robinson?'

'None that I know of. But Mildred's relatives are my relatives too.'

'Are they from around here?'

'Oh no, no. They all live in Antrim. Here, this is Mildred's best friend, Muriel. She—'

'What was it like in the orphanage, Mr Robinson?'

'Oh, I'm too old to remember any of that,' he said. 'Mildred's best friend is from Ballymena—'

'What happened to your mother and father?'

'Goodness, time does fly,' he said, gathering up the photos. I looked at the clock and jumped up. I'd been there for nearly half an hour.

'Wait.' He put his hand in his jacket pocket. 'Here you are,' he said, handing me a sixpenny coin.

'No, Mr Robinson, I don't want any money.'

'Oh, but I insist, and next time you'll have to tell me all about you and your brothers and sisters. You can call me Norman if you like.'

'We're going to Bundoran on our holidays next Sunday for a week. But I'll come to see you on Saturday before I leave,' I said, thanking him very much for the sixpence. 'I'll bring some of our photographs to show you if you like.'

'That would be lovely, Sinead. You'll not forget now, will you?'

So before we left for Bundoran I visited him again, but I forgot to bring photographs. Mr Robinson had bought a beautiful cream sponge cake. He told me more stories about Mrs Robinson. He talked about the Post Office. He talked about handwriting and how you can tell loads about a person from their handwriting. But he wouldn't talk about being an orphan.

'I have to go now Mr Robinson. I'll call again after my holidays.'

I might have been expecting him to hand me another sixpence. Or even a shilling. And I was planning to refuse. What I wasn't expecting was the pound note he took out of his pocket.

'Here you go,' he said, giving it to me. 'You can have a few extra rides on the b-b-bumper cars with that.'

'No, no, Mr Robinson. I can't …'

I didn't know what to say because he just squashed it into my hand. I didn't want him to start stuttering again. I had to take it whether I liked it or not. What choice did I have? I hadn't asked for it. No one could say I was mooching. It would have hurt his feelings if I hadn't accepted in the end. So I thanked him and said goodbye at least three times. I was just bolting his back gate when I turned to find Niamh in the lane gawking at me.

'You're in trouble, Sinead. Mammy's been looking for you. What were you doing in there?'

'I was visiting … and it's none of your business.'

Mammy was standing at the back door when I reached the house with Niamh traipsing behind me.

'Sinead, get in here this minute please!'

Mammy says she can always tell from someone's face when they're lying to her. She says sometimes people believe their own lies. I'd been planning to tell her about my visits to Mr Robinson and about the thruppence and the sixpence, but I'd forgotten to. That didn't mean I'd been lying or keeping secrets. People forget things all the time, don't they? So halfway up the path I started explaining to her about the honeysuckle and the money and the cream cake and the photos and how Mr Robinson had a lovely clean house and a piano and how he talked about Mrs Robinson like she wasn't dead and how poor Mr Robinson was an orphan and lived all alone and was lonely and I felt sorry for him and I had to take the money because I had no choice and I was saving it for Bundoran and I'd been meaning to tell her but just forgot.

Mammy didn't take me by the ear, or smack me on the legs, or tell me to get into the house straight away. Instead, she stayed dead quiet the whole time, so quiet that my face had gradually turned beetroot. When she finally did speak her voice was low. Kind almost.

'You know better than to be going to people's houses and taking money from strangers. Give me the pound note and go get the coins. We'll have to return the money to Mr Robinson after we get back from Bundoran.'

That was it. Nothing more was said and she went back to being silent. There was no use trying to explain that Mr Robinson was not a stranger. That he was a friend. A good friend.

So I went to Bundoran, stayed in a caravan all day because it rained the whole time, rode on the bumper cars a grand total of twice because the money ran out, and ended up getting a dose of the flu. But the worst thing of all was that Daddy never got to return the money to Mr Robinson, and I never got to say sorry for taking it in the first place. Because Mr Robinson was dead and buried somewhere in Antrim by the time we got back from our stupid holiday. He was lying in a hole deep in the ground, just like Granny Reilly would be in less than twenty-four hours. In the clay with worms and other creepy crawlies, creepy crawlies that squirm and wriggle their way under coffin lids into ears and up nostrils, feeding until all the flesh is gone and only the skeleton is left.

I don't feel well. I don't feel well at all.

Mammy and Daddy are coming down the stairs as I go up with the plate of stupid biscuits. They're arguing. The landing is beginning to spin.

Ashes to ashes.

The spinning speeds up.

Dust to dust.

I can't help it. I'm trying but I can't hold it in. It won't stay down. Before I can make a run for the bathroom the vomit spews all over the stairs, bits of it sticking to the flowers on the wallpaper. The custard creams are bouncing off the plate and breaking into crumbs all over the place.

I wish I was still nine.

I wish people didn't have to die.

And I wish I could go to county Antrim to put some honeysuckle on Mr Robinson's grave.

AUGUST 1969

I. Mairead

Mairead Reilly is lighting the last of the three Regal Blues she got Sinead to buy earlier with the refund on the empty lemonade bottles. Sinead had objected to carting so many bottles to the shop, especially to buy cigarettes, but Mairead hadn't wanted to use the last two shillings in her purse. Anyway, it wouldn't be happening again. She can't afford to smoke. In fact, this would be her last one. No more after that.

She has just put Michael and Eamon to bed but won't have peace and quiet to think straight until nine thirty, when the other four are settled. The blare of the *Black and White Minstrel Show* is doing her head in.

'Sinead, would you turn that sound down a wee bit! It's far too loud.'

Each shift in the hands of the clock pulls at the knot in Mairead's stomach. Paddy's never been this late before. And tonight is comic night; the children are getting restless.

Him taking on a Saturday job at the bookies might have seemed like a good idea at the time, but it's a long day when they are all off school and she has to cope on her own. At the beginning it was only going to be Saturdays. Now, it's four days a week when the schools are closed. So much for the 'long holiday advantage' of being a teacher. That's all fine and well if you don't end up having a family this size. Now, as if she didn't have enough on her plate, Paddy has taken to popping into the pub for a pint. It's becoming a habit, a bad habit, and she's going to have to do something about it. She can't, she won't, accept that Paddy is not a teetotaller – no one was more against drinking than Paddy after all the heartbreak his brother Brendan had put the whole family through.

What got into Paddy after his mother's funeral Mairead would never know. If only she had gone back down later. And what was Eileen thinking of, standing by and saying nothing? He wasn't fit to mount the stairs when he got back, and he was as sick as a dog the next day. The stink of whiskey hung in the bedroom for days. He swore he'd never let another drop of alcohol pass his lips. Mairead had every reason to believe him; who in their right mind would want to put their body through that again?

A wave of nausea flows over her. Fortunately, it settles almost immediately.

She shouldn't have refused to do it this morning. But it hadn't crossed her mind that he might get upset, especially since she'd been more than willing last night. Of course, there's no way of knowing with Paddy, is there? Sometimes he understands. This morning though, he'd been aloof at breakfast and he'd left without saying goodbye.

Is there something wrong with her? Maybe she *is* frigid,

like he says. Since Paddy started drinking she's definitely become more reluctant. Not that he drinks that much, if she's being honest about it. But he changes when he's drinking, even with a few in him. He gets a bit rough. Paddy says it's normal and that she needs to be less uptight. How would he know what's normal and what isn't? Wasn't he a virgin too when they got married?

Only when the cigarette butt threatens to burn her lips does Mairead take a final drag and throw it on to the dying cinders. There is no need for a fire in the summer months but she always lights one on Saturday to heat the boiler. If she was to use the immersion heater on the children's bath day it would cost a fortune.

'Sinead, I'm scooting over to Aunty Eileen's for five minutes to borrow a drop of milk.'

Sinead can be a strange child at times. A bit of a dreamer. Just like her father.

'When will Daddy be back?

'I don't know,' Mairead replies, buttoning her cardigan.

It makes a pleasant change to see the other three playing quietly for once. Niall and Niamh are grateful that Kieran has agreed to play marbles with them. Kieran swings from teasing his brothers and sisters to ignoring them. He thinks that being the eldest gives him license to dictate, especially since starting at the boys' grammar school. It's not an endearing trait and Mairead has had to pull him up on it once too often.

She grabs her purse and steps over them to get to the front door.

'When's Daddy coming back with our comics?' Niall pipes up, without lifting his eyes from the marble he's targeted.

Mairead pretends not to hear him and closes the front door behind her.

Despite the humidity, there's a nip in the air. She could cut across the Green, but an earlier drizzle has dampened the grass so she takes the long way round. As usual, Eileen has the key in the front door and Mairead lets herself in.

'How's it going, Aunty Mairead?'

Eileen's eldest, Mickey, is sitting at the table with a plate of poached egg on toast and a mug of tea.

'Grand, Mickey. Where is everyone?'

'The wee ones are in bed, Geraldine is still at the Mill, and the twins are down in Donoghue's, I think. Dunno where Marty is,' Mickey says, taking a gulp of tea. He has his ear semi-glued to the wireless.

'They're still rioting like mad in the Bogside, so they are, and there's talk of the British army being sent over,' Mickey says.

He's an oddball, Mickey. Not a brain in his head. But he knows everything that's happening inside and outside the country. Half the time he's talking through his hat – he believes any rumour out there. As if the British army is going to be shipped over to Northern Ireland!

'I very much doubt it'll come to that, Mickey. Where's your mother?'

'She's out at the clothes line. But the RUC can't handle the riots. You wait and see, Aunty Mairead. The army's on its way.'

'Ach, Mickey, it'll all blow over soon enough. Anyway, how was work?'

Paddy had got Mickey a full-time job at the bookies.

'I'm not long back. Leo kept us after closing – to do the books.'

Mairead takes a half step in the direction of the table.

'Ah, that's why Paddy's not home yet. I was wondering what had happened.'

But Mickey's keeping his head bent over the plate, scooping loose pieces of egg on to his toast. There'll be no information volunteered, that's obvious. And Mairead won't be asking any questions either.

Leaving Mickey to finish his supper, she enters the scullery just as Eileen is coming in through the back door with the empty clothes basket.

'Oh, you frightened me there. Is everything okay?' Eileen asks, in a pronounced sort of way.

Is she annoyed for some reason? It's hard to tell what goes on in her head sometimes.

'Yeah, everything's fine,' Mairead answers.

Eileen turns and bends over to put the empty basket into the cupboard under the sink. One of her curlers is about to fall. Her hair is far too short and brittle.

'It's just I was wondering if you could lend me a few shillings till tomorrow,' Mairead goes on apologetically. 'I thought Paddy would be home by now and I want to run to the shop. I need a couple of things for the breakfast tomorrow.'

Eileen has ignored the reference to Paddy being late home. No surprises there.

'God, Mairead, I haven't a penny to spare till payday,' she says, straightening her spine and tightening her thin lips across prominent teeth. The familiar frown follows suit. 'Wouldn't you know? Gerard went and spent a whole pile of money on more fishing tackle. I'm still bloody fuming! We're not speaking. I had to get this week's shopping on tick and I still owe for last week. I was mortified.' She looks demonic now, with the hair pin between her teeth as she tries to tighten the mutinous curler. 'Oh, but hang on, sure I clean forgot it's Mickey's payday. He should be able to lend you a few bob,' she says, heading for the living room.

It's so embarrassing being put in this position. Paddy should be ashamed of himself. Eileen doesn't know the half of it. Mairead has a good mind to show him up for what he's doing to the children. But instead she keeps her mouth shut and takes the two shillings from Eileen's outstretched hand.

'Thanks, I'll get it back to you after Mass tomorrow.'

'Ach, it's time enough till next week.'

Eileen reaches for the kettle and moves to the sink.

'Are the children all on their own? You probably don't have time for a cup of tea if you have to run to the shop.'

There it is, the implied inadequacy.

'Yes, you're right. I'd better get a move on. See you tomorrow. Bye,' says Mairead, exiting the scullery for the back entrance.

She'd be more grateful for the extra coins in her purse if she didn't feel so incompetent compared to Eileen.

It shouldn't take more than fifteen minutes to get to the shop and back if she hurries. The brisk walk does nothing to settle her, but at least Nora Diver is nowhere in sight when Mairead enters the shop. The place is empty, so she can get in and out quickly.

'Ten Regal Blues and a box of matches, Roisin.'

'Do you want the comics as well, Mrs Reilly?' Roisin asks, reaching up for the cigarettes.

The flamin' comics.

'No, I'll pick them up tomorrow after Mass.'

Roisin Diver is another busybody. Like mother like daughter.

Mairead takes the back lane home, tearing the cellophane off the cigarette packet. She slips the coupon into her cardigan pocket and tugs at the silver paper, almost pulling the whole lot out of their pack before managing to secure the filter between her fingers. The benefits of the nicotine are kicking in by the time she turns the key in her front door. The children look disappointed when they see it's not their father.

She heads straight for the scullery, turns the oven off where she has been keeping Paddy's dinner warm, and waits for a while before telling the children it's time for bed. The anticipated protest comes but she's firm with them. It isn't her fault their father is so irresponsible. No doubt he'll come up with some fancy story to explain his way out of it. He shouldn't make promises he can't keep. He's always raising their hopes and making things up to get them excited. He's such a charmer, so he is.

If only people knew what he can be like, especially when he's jealous. Jesus, Mary and Saint Joseph, he's so bloody possessive, and for the life of her she can't fathom why. She rarely goes anywhere on her own and most of the time she looks like she's been pulled through a hedge backwards. She hasn't the time to bless herself, never mind get all dolled up for men to fancy her. So what, if sometimes when they're out she gets a bit of attention, the odd admiring stare? Sure where's the harm in that? And just because she's sociable doesn't mean she's being flighty. It's not in her nature to be rude when people talk to her, men or women. The problem is that Paddy's got such strong principles and is very critical of philandering men, which isn't a bad thing, not really. Wouldn't it be worse if he was indifferent? And he's not jealous all the time.

But that's not the problem now. Paddy's drinking is the problem, or at least a potential one. Paddy can get het up as much as he wants about her making such a big deal out of it, and maybe she *is* being paranoid, but better safe than sorry. She's going to have to put her foot down, nip things in the bud, and that's the height of it.

She's down to her last two cigarettes when the car pulls up outside. No need to look at the clock to know it's well after midnight. She's sitting by the fireplace, freshly lit cigarette in hand, when the front door closes and Paddy walks into the living room. He leaves the house keys on the table.

'What are you doing up?' he asks.

The scream pushing at her throat stays down.

'You've a bloody nerve, sauntering in at this time of the night as if nothing's wrong' is the best she can manage.

Paddy says nothing for what seems like ages. He takes the car key out of his jacket pocket and purposefully drops it into the empty Belleek vase on the table. He knows damned well the metal could crack the delicate porcelain. It's her favourite ornament too. But no, that doesn't seem to concern him at all. He's taken off his jacket and placed it in the crook of his arm, like the king's butler.

'Ach for the love of God, Mairead, if you're going to start a fight I'm off to bed. I've had a long day,' he says, now moving towards the scullery.

He can try all he likes to camouflage the slur but she's not stupid. What does he take her for anyway? She's standing now, looking at him. The sparse tufts of hair sticking up near the crown of his head look comical. Not like him to miss that, with the amount of time he spends checking the miserable strands are in place.

She extinguishes her cigarette and is sitting on the armchair by the TV, arms folded, when he comes back into the living room with a pint of water in his hand.

'Well, are you going to tell me or not?' she says calmly.

It's important to curtail her anger. Paddy doesn't respond well to aggression and she needs to make him see how this new behaviour of his is simply not acceptable.

'Tell you what?'

How dare he think he can speak to her in that tone. Again she pushes down the mounting frustration.

'What do you mean, *tell you what*? I'd like to see you if *I* came home at half twelve at night.'

He's leaning against the sideboard, sipping from his glass, jacket still in the crook of his arm. Only a saint could tolerate this level of arrogance.

'Where the hell have you been? No doubt down in bloody Murphy's Bar with those so-called friends of yours. The children sat for hours waiting for their comics and I had to throw your dinner out.'

If only she could control the sharpness in her voice. But it's impossible. When he throws his jacket over the back of the couch, sets down the half-empty glass and takes off his glasses she knows the weary nose pinch and eye massage routine will follow and every part of her being wants to punch him in the face.

'There's no point in talking when you're obviously angry, Mairead,' he says after a moment of silence, broken only by the sound of the scrunched-up empty cigarette packet bouncing off the grate. 'You're not going to listen to anything I say, so I'm going on to bed,'

The burning in her eyes keeps the pent-up emotion in check. Between the inhales and exhales of her last cigarette she bites into the flesh on her cheek. There's no penetrating his alcohol-fuelled indifference but she can't just let him turn his back on her like this.

'That's right, you go on off to bed and pretend you've done nothing wrong. But you'd better start thinking what you're going to tell the children when they wake up to no comics. Some father you've become, that's all I can say.'

The minute the words are out she despises herself. The twisted smile on Paddy's face speaks for itself; she can stick the knife in all she wants but it won't make one iota of difference. Paddy couldn't care less.

'You leave the children to me. They'll be fine. Concentrate on getting that temper of yours under control,' he says, leaving the living room to go upstairs.

As soon as she hears the bedroom door closing, the tears come. Sitting on the settee, she covers her face with a cushion to muffle the sobs. When the first, uncontrollable surge of emotion is spent, she removes the cushion and heads for the bathroom, where she allows the weeping to take its course into eventual quietude. She sits on the toilet seat until the skin on her face becomes dry and taut from the salt. She then wets the face cloth and rubs it hard over her cheeks and eyes before heading back to the living room where she pulls a blanket from the hot press. Turning off the light, she lies down on the settee fully dressed and stares into the dying embers until her eyelids eventually shut out the stale, smoke-filled darkness.

II. Paddy

Paddy has been drifting in and out of sleep since dawn. He'd woken with a punch to his gut and a thumping in his head. What did he expect? He's an amateur – only hardened drinkers like Danny Lynch can sidestep hangovers.

That first moment of disorientation is the worst, his brain trying to unscramble abstract images until memory allows snippets of coherent recollection to filter through.

I didn't do anything I shouldn't have with Grainne Cunningham ... we were only chatting ... I couldn't just get up and leave with two rounds of drink still in front of me and my turn to buy before closing ... Mairead has become a full-time nag ... she's turning into my bloody mother.

With this clarity of mind, the initial intensity of physical discomfort subsides, though his brain only lets him slip into doze mode.

When Sinead comes into the bedroom quite late, on this morning of all mornings, Paddy's face is buried under the blankets and he pretends to be asleep. If he could, he'd stay in bed. But it's Sunday, time for eleven o'clock Mass. God forbid that a man who works six days a week can have a lie-in on a Sunday.

'Daddy, Mammy says you have to get up.'

Sinead's voice triggers a flutter of anxiety. He has no comics and no money left to buy them. But it's not his fault he had to lend Danny Lynch five quid. He could hardly have refused, not when Danny had stood an extra round.

Sinead is not for leaving, but there's no way he can face going to eleven o'clock Mass. He'll go to the half twelve. The four of them are old enough to walk to Mass on their own now. Mairead could have told them that. Poking his head out from under the covers he's forced to adopt an uncharacteristic authoritarian tone to tell Sinead what her mother should have told her. Then he makes a point of ducking further under the sheets. But sleep has well and truly done a runner.

When the children leave the house and the girls' chatter has faded, he throws back the blankets. Sitting on the edge of the bed, he waits for the pounding in his head to ease off a bit before pulling his pyjamas out from under the pillow. Forever the optimist, he had jumped into bed last night naked and contrite. Wishful thinking. Mairead must have slept on the couch, again.

All morning he's been hovering between temptation and the fear of sinking into the shame that always comes after giving in to it. But now, only a need to pee stops him from getting back into bed and succumbing. He wouldn't have a problem at all if Mairead was more willing. It's not natural for a man of his age to have to demean himself, but it's like he's in constant combat with the devil himself. Anyway, this time he's knocked the devil for six and the devil had better get used to it. Paddy has willpower as much as the next man.

His headache is lifting. He crosses the bedroom to the dressing table mirror where he straightens and presses the hair onto his scalp with the help of saliva. Comics first thing after Mass, definitely. Mrs Diver won't mind putting them on the tab until next Saturday. There's no reason for Mairead to find out. Mrs Diver will understand.

It's a novelty to find the living room so peaceful. The sun has made its way round to the front window and is illuminating toast crusts on piece plates. Emptied cups of tea are clustered in the centre of the table. But there's a pungent smell of fresh wax coming from the linoleum under his bare feet, a sure sign that Mairead hasn't slept much. It's only then, for the first time this morning, that another unwelcome emotion creeps in: dread. It's never too far from the surface in situations like these.

What should he expect? A berating or the silent treatment? Hopefully, she'll speak to him. He's feeling genuinely repentant. He should have come on home and brought the comics like he was supposed to. What gets into him sometimes? He just loses track of time, especially when the craic is good.

Lifting an orphaned Lego piece en route, he goes into the empty scullery. Outside, at the back garden gate, Mairead is talking to Rita Donoghue. Baby Michael is close by and tumbles on the grass, trying to chase the ball which Eamon has just kicked into the hedge. Where did Eamon get those splay-feet from?

Before crossing the hall to get to the bathroom, Paddy checks that the back door isn't wide open. Mairead might not be facing the house, but Rita Donoghue never misses a bar, and he doesn't want her to be getting an eyeful of him in pyjamas when he crosses the back hall to go into the bathroom. Luckily, the door is shut tight.

Safely inside the bathroom, he turns the key in the lock and quickly relieves himself before going over to the sink. Better to wash and shave and then have breakfast. He's ravenous now. Not surprising. He hasn't eaten a bite since lunchtime yesterday. No wonder the drink went straight to his head. Let that be a lesson learned.

Filling the washbasin, he takes his shaving brush and razor from the cupboard. Plain soap beats shaving cream any day of the week. Plus it's far cheaper. Keeps the skin looking fresher too.

Mairead's voice carries across the scratching of the razor blade and the running tap.

'Eamon, keep an eye on your brother!'

The chatting is over. She'll be back into the house any moment now. His hand is trembling from the hunger and lack of sleep. Scraps of tissue paper are stuck on blood spots where he's managed to nick himself five times so far. The back door squeaks and he turns the tap on full. Best that she knows he's up and getting ready for Mass. When he finally braves it back into the scullery, Mairead is standing in front of the cooker browning the Sunday roast. She neither lifts her eyes nor speaks. Nothing for him to do but loiter at the sink and peer out the window. He has a bit of a druth so he pours himself a glass of water.

'That smells good,' he says between long sips.

He tries again.

'Leo kept us late last night to do the books. I had to do the final tallying and I'll tell you one thing for nothing – he's making some money!'

He empties the remaining water and sets the glass down. Then he turns his back to the window and leans against the sink, arms folded. It looks as if she's about to say something when the panicky voice of Eamon breaks the silence.

'Mammy, Mammy, Michael wants to eat a worm!'

Mairead turns off the gas ring and rushes past Paddy, accidentally nipping his left foot. Turning back to face the window again, he watches her swoop Michael up and scoop what might or might not be a worm from his mouth. Paddy's stomach is more than a bit queasy now. He has to get food into him.

Michael is screeching in protest as Mairead pulls him along the garden path towards the house.

'Go to your father and stop that crying,' she orders, entering the scullery.

Paddy reaches down to lift him up.

'Hey dopey, what have you been up to? Only birdies eat worms. Come on, let's get that face washed and then you can help Daddy get ready for Mass.'

Mairead isn't biting, as is plain to see from her stern profile. Isn't it funny how even when she's angry and in bad form she's still so attractive? Attractive, but as cold as an iceberg. For God's sake, he came home a bit late. So what? He could see through it if he was out every night of the week. Why does she always have to make a mountain out of a measly molehill, always preaching about this or that? She didn't use to be so uptight. Fair enough, it's not easy having six children to run after, but he does what he can. It's not easy for him either, teaching all day and then having to help run the community centre three evenings a week. Not many men hand in every penny they earn and have to hold down a Saturday job for pocket money. He's entitled to a night out. Doesn't she go to the bingo?

No point asking for something to eat, and since she's obviously not planning to make him any breakfast, he'll just have to go without. He holds Michael over the sink, washes the dirt off his face and dries him with the tea towel. He then tucks him under his arm and hauls him into the living room, calling out at the top of his voice, 'Boy for sale! Boy for sale!' which has Michael giggling in no time. They climb the stairs together.

'Now sit there like a good boy till Daddy gets ready for Mass.'

But there's a dirty nappy nagging at his nostrils, so Paddy gets dressed quickly.

'Come on, boyo! Let's get that bum cleaned. Did you forget to ask Mammy for the potty?'

He carries Michael downstairs, pulls a nappy from the hot press, changes him, making sure to apply plenty of ointment, and plonks him on the couch with a pile of old comics. He's checking his jacket for the car key when Sinead and Niamh walk in, back from eleven o'clock Mass.

'Where are the boys?' he asks.

Sinead ignores him but Niamh comes over to where he's standing.

'They've gone over to Marty's. Have you got our comics, Daddy?' she asks.

'Mrs Diver hadn't got them ready but I'll be calling for them after Mass, okay pet?'

Sometimes a wee white lie doesn't harm anyone.

Mairead is talking to Sinead and her words travel loud and clear into the living room.

'Tell your father to get a half pint of fresh cream on his way back.'

When Mairead resorts to the tell-your-father tactic, it's a fair indicator she won't be speaking to him for a while. No one knows how to dish out the silent treatment better than she does. No, not true – his mother is the reigning queen of that, even if she is dead.

He pulls the front door shut and gets into the car. The problem now is how to get the fresh cream. He has spent whatever Leo paid him yesterday and he can't very well get it on tick at Diver's since he'll need all his credit credibility to secure two weeks' worth of comics.

He's running five minutes late by the time he parks up at the chapel, which is packed so he has to stand at the back with the other latecomers. Then he spots Vera Reilly in one of the back pews on her own. Not a good sign. Brendan only misses Mass when he's been on the tear. It's been a while since the last binge. Paddy has stayed clear since that particular debacle. If Brendan doesn't want to help himself, nobody else is going to be able to help him. How many times has Brendan declared he was for taking The Pledge? Too many times to be taken seriously.

The minute Father Duncan steps off the altar, Paddy is outside and in the car. He turns in the direction of Vera's housing estate and pulls up at the kerb to wait. He has the windows rolled down when she passes.

'Hey, Vera, do you want a lift?'

'Ach, Paddy, that's great, thanks,' she says, getting into the car. 'How come you're at this Mass?'

'I wasn't feeling the best this morning so I had a lie-in. It was a long day yesterday. How's that brother of mine getting on?' he asks, pulling away from the kerb.

'Ah, don't talk to me, Paddy. He didn't come home on Friday after work and got back in the small hours of this morning paralytic. It's a wonder he didn't wake up the whole street.'

'You should have called round at ours on Friday, Vera. I'd have gone looking for him.'

'Ach, what's the point? He's a lost cause.'

She's right. Brendan's a beaten docket, and Paddy is sick of dragging him out of empty bars. But he wouldn't want Vera to think the family has washed their hands of him. Besides, if she ever did ask for his help he wouldn't refuse.

When they stop outside her front gate she invites him in for a cup of tea. She has cream doughnuts and apple tarts. Tempting. But he needs to be getting back. Though not before he asks her one last thing.

'Hey, Vera, you wouldn't have a pound to spare until tomorrow? I've a couple of messages to get for Mairead and my money is in yesterday's trousers. It's no problem if you're short – it would just save me having to go the whole way home first, that's all.'

Vera's always good for a sub. She's a saint – there are few and far between who could be credited with her capacity for patience and kindness. No other woman would put up with Brendan. It's one thing to have a quick drink the day after you've had one too many – the hair of the dog as they say – but it's another thing entirely to drink for days and not go home. It's a shame. Brendan is the most decent man you could meet when he's sober. And he's by far the smartest in the family, even without an education. Paddy can admit to that.

'Thanks, Vera. I'll call up tomorrow.'

'That would be great, Paddy.'

The throbbing in Paddy's head is back. It hadn't actually left completely, but the pulsations have a rhythmical sharpness now that wasn't there before. And the mood he's been fending off since dawn has found a crack in his armour.

He pulls out of the estate and takes the road back down past the chapel. By the time he nears Diver's shop the blackness is threatening to flood and his breathing is becoming more laboured. Mairead should visit Vera Reilly more often. She might learn a thing or two.

Diver's is busy. He'll try one of the other shops in town. He drives down the Ballybeehan Road, crosses the bridge and turns into Delaney Street. He can park the car outside Gormley's Chemist and backtrack to Murphy's.

He's already feeling better when Harry Murphy unlatches the door to let him in.

'A quick pint, Harry, and then I'm off,' he says, as the door shuts out the light and he makes his way to the dimly lit bar.

JULY
1970

I. Sinead

Linda is coming down her front path. She looks ridiculous with all that cream on her sunburn. Like a Red Indian with war paint on. Her eyes are standing in her head and her mouth is doing an Open Sesame. She is so excited that she tries to open the gate without pulling the bolt.

'Oh, the pram is gorgeous, Sinead.'

She's petting the shiny black hood and silver handle bar – she'd better not have any of that sunburn cream on her fingers. Now she's staring at the gigantic wheels and the carrier basket underneath. She's dead jealous.

'The size of it … it's huge. Aw, doesn't Shauna look so tiny snuggled up in that fluffy blanket,' she whispers. At least she has the sense to keep her voice down.

'This is her first run in it. I'm allowed to take her as far as Diver's to get some bread and milk. Do you want to come?' I know full well she does. 'You can push it as far as the phone box if you like.'

'I'll have to tell Mummy. Wait there a wee minute.'

I'm not hanging around to wait for her. Honestly, she's so annoying sometimes. She'll do nothing without asking her mummy. Any time we have a fight she runs to her mammy and her mammy is always giving her advice like 'We should try to see the other person's side of things' or 'We should always discuss things'. Could you see my mammy going on like that? I suppose if Mrs Dunne had seven children instead of two she wouldn't have the time to be sitting around yapping so much. Protestants don't have a whole pile of wains like us Catholics. I think it's because they don't have a pope.

'I've no time to wait, Linda. Sure we're only going to the shop.'

Finally, a decision without running to her mammy.

She's dying to push the pram. It's obvious. I can't tell if she's jealous of us having a new baby or a new pram. Both, probably. Though the pram's not brand, brand new. Mammy bought it off Mrs Arbuckle whose baby died. It's a very expensive make, but we got it for a bargain.

'Not so fast, Linda! We have to watch for stones – they can get caught in the spokes.'

She's not the greatest at keeping the pram straight.

'Here, I'd better push it. You can have another go on the way back.'

It's okay for her to be jealous for a change. Now she knows what it's like.

I don't know why I get so jealous. I shouldn't. My daddy is a teacher and all her daddy does is drive a lorry. And she didn't get to dress up for Confirmation or First Holy Communion and collect so much money. But still, I can't help being jealous of her. I'm mostly jealous of her house. It always looks so smart and tidy. And she has her own bedroom. And Mrs Dunne is always baking scones and angel cakes. Plus she gets far more Easter eggs than me, and I hate it when she shows them to me, all lined up on her dressing table. Imagine? She's got her own dressing table. You can't swing a cat in me and Niamh's room with Shauna's cot stuck up against the wall.

Another thing too that's been annoying me recently about Linda is that she's becoming a show-off. She thinks she's the bee's knees because she's started wearing a bra. If you ask me she doesn't need it. Even if she is a year older, her diddies are hardly any size at all.

'We have to go the long way round through Croghan Drive. Mammy says there are too many boulders and holes down the back lane.'

I have to be extra careful tilting the pram off the pavement to cross the road, which is definitely something Linda wouldn't have a clue how to do.

'Linda, could you let go of the handlebar please?' She probably thinks she's helping me keep the pram straight.

'Can I not push it for a bit now, Sinead?'

'Maybe on the way back.'

Did she not hear me the first time?

I'm trying to keep my voice calm in case she starts bawling her eyes out again. She's always been a bit of a crybaby, but lately I'm afraid to open my mouth. It's because of the Carrickfergus thing, though I think she's exaggerating as usual. I told her this the last time she got all sniffly.

'I mean, Linda, don't you think you're exaggerating a bit?' I'd said. 'Your daddy might not get a job in Carrickfergus. Even if he does, it's still not for sure he'll take it. Didn't he say he likes his job here and doesn't want to leave? Your mammy might change her mind.'

'No chance,' was all she could say. It was lucky I had an old tissue in my pocket because the snots had started. Her mammy doesn't want to live in a Catholic town any more – at least, that's what Linda told me.

'Hey, I didn't tell you about my cousins' christening,' I say now to change the subject.

'No, you didn't.'

It's her huffy voice.

'Aw, the twins were lovely, so they were. They didn't cry the once, not even when Father Duncan poured the holy water over their heads. They slept the whole time we were at the hotel.'

I leave out the part where Uncle Brendan had an argument with Daddy, who was a bit tipsy. There's no harm in that, according to Daddy. But Uncle Brendan has taken The Pledge and is death on the drink now.

Linda's never been to a hotel for her lunch.

'The food was class. We had vooloovonts, and all sorts of things I don't know the name of. Do you know what a vooloovont is?'

'Mummy bakes vol-au-vents all the time.'

Yeah, right.

'What are Protestant christenings like?' I can't think of anything else to say to her.

'I haven't been to one. I was only two when my cousin from Carrickfergus …'

She goes all quiet again. Thank goodness we're almost at Diver's.

There are three boys sitting on the wall across from the shop. I know one of them: Joe Duffy. He's two years older than Kieran, and Mammy and Daddy don't allow Kieran to talk to him. Or to any of the Duffy boys. They're constantly getting into trouble with the RUC or spitting at the British army patrols. The other two boys must be from the head of the town because I've never seen them before. I've not been up the head of the town for ages. I'm too scared because of the stone-throwing that goes on up there.

The pram's too big to bring into the shop.

'Keep an eye on the pram until I get the messages.'

But Linda's not for doing any such thing.

'I'm coming inside. I can keep an eye from there.'

She's eyeballing Diver's dog sound asleep over in the corner.

'Linda, Diver's dog is a hundred years old. There's nothing to be scared of. It can hardly walk, and it wouldn't hurt a fly.'

'Okay, but hurry up.'

I swear to God I don't know what she'd do without me. I mean, she won't even go to the ice cream van on her own. It's always me who has to do the paying and asking for things. Not that it bothers me though, because Linda pays for me a lot of the time when Mammy has no money to spare. Which is nearly always, I suppose. Linda gets proper pocket money for doing chores for her mammy and daddy, if drying the dishes or keeping her room tidy can be called chores. If I lived in her house, I'd be a millionaire by now. I've been cooking, washing, waxing lino, ironing and a whole pile more since no age and the most I get is a cream bun. But you know something? Even if Mammy could afford to pay me I wouldn't take the money. Linda's forever reciting the Ten Commandments but what about the most important commandment of all – 'Help others as you expect others to help you'? At least, I think it's one of the commandments. Mammy says it often enough.

Today, though, I can buy Linda a gobstopper because I'm allowed to keep the change from the messages. That will cheer her up.

'Do you want the purple one or the red one?' I ask, holding out the paper bag after I've put the bread and milk into the carrier part of the pram.

She's delighted. 'Oh thanks, Sinead. Can I have the red one?'

We toss the gobstoppers into our mouths at the same time.

My gobstopper is just starting to roll about in lots of juicy spit when all of a sudden a stone bounces off the metal on the hood of the pram and hits Linda on the top of her arm. She squeals and her gobstopper shoots out of her mouth on to my T-shirt. Her face is all twisted. She's squeezing her arm and there's a disgusting, red dribble sliding down the freckles on her chin. I've hardly time to think, and the next thing I know there are more stones. One of them hits me so hard on the side of my knee that my gobstopper gets stuck for a second in my throat before I cough it back up and catch it in my hand. Linda is screaming now and runs to the other side of the pram where she hunkers down to escape the stones.

I turn around. The three heads of the boys go down behind the wall they'd been sitting on.

'You just wait till I tell my daddy what you're up to. We'll see if you act the hard men then,' I shout.

But to tell you the truth I'm scared out of my wits. And I'm raging with Linda for using our pram to escape the stones.

'Linda, make a run for it,' I yell, pointing to the back lane.

I have to yell a second time, louder, before she takes me on. She nearly trips over herself because she's trying to run bent over with her hands covering her head. She's nearly turned into the lane when Joe Duffy jumps up over the wall and starts walking towards her. Linda is no Speedy Gonzales so I have to scream at her a third time.

'Run faster, Linda!'

Then she lets out a screech that I'm surprised the whole town doesn't hear.

Joe Duffy stops outside the first house on the lane and turns to look at me.

'That's what you get for going around with Protestants, Sinead Reilly.'

But he's going back over to the other two boys.

Thank God they're heading towards the shortcut into town.

I'm pushing like an eejit, but the pram won't budge because the brake is still on and by the time I figure this out Shauna has woken up and is crying. I fiddle about for her dummy, lick the fluff of it, stick it in her mouth, flick the brake and start running for the lane. Mrs Diver has come out of the shop. *Now* she wants to know what's going on.

'Nothing, Mrs Diver.'

I'm not for hanging about in case the boys change their minds and come after me and Linda. It's a wonder no one else has heard the rumpus – all the windows of the houses are wide open.

Jeepers, my heart is pumping. That Joe Duffy is a bad egg. I'm going to tell Daddy to go to the police. Luckily I had the hood of the pram up or Shauna might have got hit. There's a dent in the metal, and even if I know it's not my fault, Mammy is going to lose the bap. She might not let me take the pram out again. It's not fair. Linda was so stupid hiding behind the pram like that. And I shouldn't be going home this way. The wheels keep jamming.

I'm still shaking a wee bit when Linda suddenly appears from behind McGonigle's fence.

'Shite, you frightened the living day lights out of me!' Trust Linda to make me swear. I could kill her.

But then I see her blotchy face. She's still half crying. Ach, and her shorts are damp where she's wet herself. She must be broke to the bone. I'd be mortified too if I were her.

'They're gone, Linda. Don't be afraid. And that Joe Duffy is going to be in big trouble by the time I'm finished telling Daddy what happened.'

'No, no, Sinead. You mustn't do that. Promise. What if the police come to our house? I should have told Mummy where I was going. If she asks me where I was I'll tell her, but only if she asks me. That's not the same as lying, is it?'

'No, that's definitely not the same as lying.'

Of course it's the same as lying. That's why you have confession. No one is allowed to have secrets. Well, not Catholics anyway. But maybe Protestants are allowed to keep secrets because they don't have confession. Or mortal sins. So then Linda's probably right. It's not the same as lying – if you're a Protestant.

'Oh, look at the hood. What's your mummy going to say when she sees that?'

'She probably won't even notice it.'

Now that's a definite lie. Miracles can happen, but not when it comes to expensive things like our new pram. I'm feeling so sorry for her now that I can't let on I'll have to tell Mammy some of the truth if she asks me, though I'll not say it was Joe Duffy in case Daddy does go to the RUC and they land on Linda's doorstep.

'Come on, let's go. Do you want to push the pram a bit?'

'No, it's okay. I'm not in the mood.'

I try again but it's no use. She just shakes her head and I can't get a peep out of her the rest of the way.

'Do you want to play out on the Green after dinner?'

'I don't know.' She's pulling at the bolt on her front gate. 'Okay.'

Halfway up her front path she turns and waves.

'Bye.'

'Bye.'

I want to tell her that she mustn't be such a scaredy-cat all the time. But instead I just wave back and push the pram home.

II. Mairead

'Sinead! What happened to the pram?'

Mairead is standing at the back door looking out on to the garden, where Sinead is hunkered down gathering honeysuckle from their overgrown hedge.

'What do you mean, Mammy?' Sinead calls out, straightening up.

'There's a dent on the hood. It wasn't there before you went to Diver's,' says Mairead, lifting Shauna further onto her left shoulder before marching down the garden path.

This has got to be the last of them, surely. Seven children. Not how she had imagined motherhood. She'd always assumed the pregnancies would stop at three or four. There were four in her family and three in Paddy's. The numbers had stuck.

Sinead has laid the bunch of flowers on the ground and is rubbing her hands on the side of her skirt as Mairead draws closer. Jesus, Mary and Joseph, what has she done now? In many ways, Sinead can be very childish. But she'll be starting at the grammar school in September so she needs to grow up a bit and act more responsibly.

Agitation is not going to help Mairead get to the bottom of why their new pram is almost ruined, but it's been a rough few weeks and she'd have to be super human to stay calm when things like this happen. God, it seems that the more babies you have, the more you're expected to just get on with things. It shouldn't feel like this much hard work, but it does, so it's perfectly natural that her temper gets frayed at times, isn't it?

'I don't want any lies, Sinead. Tell me what happened to the pram this minute,' she shouts.

Sinead's cheeks are blazing. Guilty as bloody sin.

'Tell me now!' Mairead screeches into Sinead's face before Sinead has a chance to speak.

'I-I d-don't know,' Sinead stammers.

'Get inside at once,' and with her free hand Mairead skelps Sinead on her bare arm as she scurries past towards the house. The jerk starts Shauna crying. Sinead is standing at the scullery sink washing her hands, and Mairead goes into the living room where she soothes Shauna by putting a dummy into her mouth before laying her in the pram. She's lucky that Shauna is such a placid baby.

Sinead has come into the living room and is leaning against the sideboard, cleaning her glasses with the hem of her skirt. Mairead waits for her to put them back on. Why do babies have to grow up?

'Look at me, Sinead, and tell me exactly how you managed to get a dent on the hood and stones in the spokes of the wheels? Didn't I tell you not to take the pram down the back lane? Didn't I?' she says, allowing a hint of pity to creep into her words.

Sinead's shoulders straighten and she takes an involuntary step forward.

'It wasn't my fault, Mammy. It was Linda's fault. If she hadn't hidden behind the pram, it wouldn't have happened. I shouted at her to run but she didn't listen, and then by the time she made a run for it, it was too late. I didn't want to go up the back lane but that Joe Duffy … I mean those boys …'

'Wait, slow down. What has Joe Duffy got to do with anything?'

Mairead's stomach sinks. Sinead has retreated to the sideboard and lowered her eyes again.

'I can't tell you because I promised Linda I wouldn't in case Daddy goes to the RUC and they land on Linda's doorstep.'

Good God Almighty, what next!

Mairead leads Sinead back into the scullery. Michael and Eamon are watching *Magic Roundabout* and the other two are out on the Green. Kieran and Paddy shouldn't be back from the hospital for at least half an hour. Hopefully the consultant in Derry can sort out Kieran's problem and they won't have to trek to Belfast. Just this once she doesn't mind if Paddy gets home even later – he plans to call with Danny Lynch on the way back to supposedly talk about getting Kieran into art.

Paddy and his notions. As if art is going to help Kieran with his seizures, or keep him from getting into trouble. More like an excuse for Paddy to spend more time out of the house with his drinking buddy. Danny Lynch might be a great art teacher but he's a heavy drinker and a bad influence on Paddy.

'Listen, Sinead, you have to tell me everything. No one's going to be running to the RUC.'

Sinead looks up and starts crying. Through the sobs she tells Mairead how the three boys had thrown stones and called Linda names and how Linda had wet herself and that Joe Duffy was a no-good git. By the time she finishes, the tears are subsiding and her hands have formed rigid fists which she's pressing into her sides.

'I'm sorry about the pram, Mammy. I went to the shop the long way through Croghan Drive like you told me to. I didn't mean to come home by the back lane but I was just following Linda.'

The fists unfold into open palms once again.

'It's fine. Forget about it now. Listen to me, say nothing to your father or Kieran about this.' Paddy can sometimes be impulsive. 'Did anyone else see what went on?'

'I don't think so. Maybe Mrs Diver. I don't know. She came out but the boys had cleared off by then.'

'Okay. I'm going to go down to Mrs Dunne to have a word. You stay here with the wee ones until I get back, and if your daddy gets home before me, just say I've gone for a message. Do you hear me? You say nothing.'

The confusion and fear in Sinead's eyes force Mairead to slow down and keep her emotions in check. Sinead is too perceptive for her years, too much in tune with Mairead's thoughts and feelings. But she can't explain something to Sinead that she's incapable of explaining to herself. What's happening to this town, this neighbourhood? And the Duffys – they're to be feared. They've always been rough, but their status on the estate has taken on a sinister quality since the start of the Troubles. Paddy can say what he likes but everyone knows that Riordan Duffy has got connections in the IRA.

'Sinead, are you listening?'

'Yes, Mammy, I won't tell anyone,' Sinead replies in a flat voice.

'There's nothing to be worried about. I'm going to sort it out, okay?' Mairead says, disappearing out the back door.

The empty clothes line is a reminder of the overflowing wash basket in the bathroom. She doesn't mind the washing so much; it's the ironing that's the problem. She invariably delays putting a load on until the ironing basket is empty. Lately she's been lazy, ironing bits and pieces as they're needed. The heap of unironed clothes is an eyesore every time she opens the hot press. She shouldn't have bothered with bingo last night. But the Snowball was over a hundred pounds and Paddy had pushed her out the door. He's good like that sometimes, taking over when he sees how overworked she is.

As she pulls the back gate behind her, her tongue slides across and around her teeth. She's forgotten to brush them again. Also, the ladder in her stocking has crawled further down her leg, despite the nail varnish she'd smothered on to keep it from running. If it wasn't for her varicose veins she wouldn't have to wear bloody tights in the summer. But there's nothing she can do about it now. She just won't stand too close to Mrs Dunne, that's all.

She loiters outside Mrs Dunne's back gate for a moment before slipping in unnoticed. They've been neighbours since the estate was built but neither of them has ever had a reason to visit the other. In fact, she knows very little about this woman from Carrickfergus. Derek Dunne, on the other hand, comes from a village three miles down the road, a decent, hard-working man who supported the Civil Rights Movement. It's a disgrace that things are getting so out of hand.

She carefully closes the garden gate behind her and hurries up the gravelled path to the back door. The garden warrants her envy. No weeds, grass trimmed, colourful flower beds to break the monotonous green. Mairead's eyes skip over a tiny patch of baby shamrock before landing on the beautiful, tall hedge that secures complete privacy. Edna Dunne is lucky to have a man who takes an interest in his garden.

She doesn't have to knock. The door opens just as she's mounting the first step.

'Hello, Mrs Reilly.'

'Oh hello, Mrs Dunne. Sorry to bother you, but I was wondering if we could have a chat in private,' Mairead says, stepping back on to the path. Linda is standing behind her mother, eyes swollen; she's obviously been crying.

'Oh, it's no bother at all. Please, please, come in.'

Could Edna Dunne's teeth be any whiter?

'Ah no, I can't stop, but thanks. It's just that I've left the baby with Sinead and it's near her feeding time.'

It's rude to stare but Mairead can't help herself. The crisply ironed lilac blouse, the pleated, tweed skirt and the obviously very new patent sandals. Not what you'd call an everyday outfit. More like what Mairead would wear to go to Mass – if she had such nice clothes, that is. Protestants do dress very well.

'Your garden is really beautiful, Mrs Dunne. It puts ours to shame.'

'Oh, thank you. Derek and I love gardening, and now that the children are older I have more time to spend keeping it in shape. I sometimes forget myself, especially in the summer months, and I get nothing done in the house because of it. I'm going to miss … Linda, go back into the house.'

Mairead recognises a forced cough when she hears one and it's clear Edna Dunne is feeling uneasy when she closes the back door behind her and approaches her.

'I'm glad you called, Mrs Reilly. I've been trying to get Linda to tell me what happened. All I can make out is that some boys threw stones at Sinead and the pram, and when I told Linda I thought I should talk to you and your husband she flew into a panic.'

Mairead's heart is beating fast with relief – Linda hasn't told the truth. If Linda's parents don't find out what really happened, they won't go to the police, which means there'll be no drawing attention to anything. She's been worried about Sinead's friendship with Linda sticking out like a sore thumb. The Dunnes are the only Protestant family left on the estate. And Derek and Edna Dunne going to the RUC might be enough to tip the scales with Kieran, who has been getting caught up in all this talk about 'The Cause', reading too many books. Paddy needs to do something about it.

'Ah, now it makes sense. You see, there's a dent in the pram,' says Mairead, her eyes dropping for a second. 'Sinead says she doesn't know how it got there, but I knew she was with Linda so that's why I called with you. Sinead's probably afraid to tell me.'

Mairead must try to keep direct eye contact. Lying does not come easily, but there are times when it can't be avoided. The right words and phrases have to be juggled about in her head. Diplomacy is crucial.

'Perhaps it's best you don't push Linda to talk about it. You know what it's like at that age, being loyal and what have you. They're dying dead about each other.'

As she speaks she tries to pat down some errant hair she had intended to put in curlers when she got the chance. She hadn't planned to leave the house and has been on the go since Shauna's early morning feed.

'What I mean to say is, since they're such good friends and Sinead trusts Linda so much, it's probably best Linda knows Sinead is staying silent. And of course I won't let on to Sinead that I know about the stone-throwing.' Mairead wouldn't blame Mrs Dunne for thinking she's got a screw loose. Mairead herself is getting confused by the nonsense tumbling out of her mouth.

'I see what you mean … I think. But what should I tell Linda we were talking about?'

'Well, I suppose you'll have to tell her the truth. It's just better she doesn't talk to Sinead about it. It won't help things. Sinead doesn't know I'm here. I told her I was going for a message. But now that I'm aware of the bullying, Paddy and I will get to the bottom of it, so thanks.'

Is that a patronising expression on Edna Dunnes's face? Mairead has to get away now as quickly as possible. It's not that she doesn't appreciate the interest being shown. But there's nothing more to say to make this woman understand that from here on in they would deal with the problem themselves. Despite herself, though, Mairead can't stop talking.

'Sinead isn't the easiest of children, if the truth be told. She's stubborn and is forever getting into scraps. Sometimes I think she'd fight her own shadow if she was alone for long enough.'

Not exactly in keeping with the profile of a child who'd get bullied by a few boys.

'But deep down she's sensitive, which is maybe why she sometimes gets picked on at school. Don't be worrying yourself, Mrs Dunne. Sinead will eventually open up. And thank you so much for your help.'

There's no salvaging her dignity. She needs to shut down the babbling. Right now.

'Goodness, you don't need to be thanking me for anything, Mrs Reilly.'

Mairead is moving towards the garden gate. There's only so much a person can say about plants and flowers. Small talk comes naturally when their paths occasionally cross. But not here. Not in the intimate confines of this garden.

'I think I'll send Paddy to the library for a couple of gardening books before the weeds get any higher. Honestly, he hasn't the hands to bless himself.'

It's highly unlikely Edna Dunne will get the humour and Mairead isn't hanging around to find out. But as she hurries back home, arms folded across her ribcage, she could kick herself. Did she have to stoop to criticising Paddy, or Sinead for that matter, in front of someone she barely knows? So what if their garden doesn't come up to the standards of *Gardeners World*? Paddy helps out in other ways, though she had to say something about Sinead to cover up. Anyway, the main thing is that the problem is under control. As long as Sinead understands that it's for the best to keep the whole incident to herself from here on in, it will all soon blow over. It's at times like these that Mairead appreciates Sinead's mature side. There will be no more straying too far from sight with Linda in tow. Mairead intends to keep a close eye on the pair of them. Things are simply too dangerous at the moment.

'Good girl yourself, Sinead. Here, let me get her into the pram.'

Mairead's voice is soft. She takes Shauna from where she is sound asleep in Sinead's arms. She's due a feed but it doesn't matter. The midwives say babies should be fed on time, woken in the middle of the night if necessary, but that's a load of nonsense. All hers were weaned off the night feed within a month. A baby's stomach needs to rest.

Sinead is too quiet.

'It's all sorted. Linda hasn't told the truth about what happened. So your daddy doesn't need to know anything. It'll only worry him and there's no telling how he might react. You know what he can be like. And if Linda doesn't want her parents to know, who are we to be interfering. Okay?'

'Okay.'

'Take the wee ones outside for a bit. I need to get some ironing done. We'll get some cream buns for tea, how about that?'

'Fine.'

Michael and Eamon are already heading for the door. What would Mairead do without her?

She gets stuck into the ironing and has just stopped for a quick smoke when Paddy pulls up outside. Just as well. She's exhausted. Taking the plug from the socket she goes to the front door to warn them that Shauna is asleep. Niamh and Niall are coming inside too, ahead of Paddy, but Kieran is walking away down the estate. She can't shout out to ask where he's going but Paddy reads her mind.

'He's away over to the fields to play football.'

'Football? Since when has Kieran taken an interest in football?'

'Since five minutes ago. For God's sake, Mairead, how would I know? And just because he's not an enthusiast doesn't mean he's not interested …'

Paddy lowers his voice mid-sentence when he sees the pram. He sounds worn out. Too many hours at the flamin' bookies.

'Well? What did the consultant say?'

She orders a reluctant Niamh and Niall to go back outside and help Sinead with the wee ones until she calls them for dinner.

'He's referring him for tests and an EEG.'

'What's that?'

'It's an electroencephalogram. They put metal discs on the scalp to monitor brain activity. The consultant thinks the seizures might be because of something called petit mal, which can happen in the teenage years and which goes away with time. We'll see, but he doesn't seem to think it's anything to worry about.'

Nothing to worry about? Is he serious? What else is she going to hear today? But she lets it go. Now isn't the right time.

'Well, I'm sure the doctor knows what he's talking about. Do you want a cup of tea?'

'No, I'm all right,' he answers, falling into the armchair.

'Is there something you're not telling me?' she ventures.

'God, Mairead, what would I not be telling you? I'm knackered, that's all. It was a nightmare getting to the hospital. The army's stopping everyone and detouring cars. The Union Jacks are flying full mast in preparation for the Twelfth parades. You'd think after what happened last year they'd tone it down a bit.'

'But you can't expect them to give up their tradition just because things have got a bit out of control. It would be like us not being able to march on Saint Patrick's Day.'

'It's not the same thing.'

She has to kill this line of conversation; Sinead has just walked in.

'Saint Patrick's Day is a religious tradition,' he goes on. 'This is different. Orangemen all over the country are becoming fanatical. They're playing with fire. No one enjoys watching the parades more than me, but people need to calm down – at least until the country comes to its senses. Even Derek Dunne agrees – who, by the way, is moving to Carrickfergus. He's got a new job. I gave him a lift from town.'

'Oh, really? That's a pity. When are they leaving?'

'He'll be starting at the beginning of next month.'

Sinead is heading for the door.

'Where are you going, Sinead?' Mairead calls after her.

'Upstairs to read my book.'

'She's going to miss Linda,' Paddy whispers.

'She'll be fine. Her and Linda aren't as close as they used to be.'

Mairead turns on her heels and heads for the scullery. They'll have to make do with tea and sandwiches. She can't face cooking today.

OCTOBER
1970

I. Paddy

It's hard to say no to Danny Lynch.

'No more after this one, Danny – you'll have me on my ear.'

The two stiff glasses of vodka Paddy has downed have seeped into every sinew of his body, a welcome heat against the October cold. His ears were numb by the time he arrived at Danny's. What possessed him to leave without his hat and coat?

Paddy shoots a glance across the room to where Kieran has stood back from the easel to examine his painting.

'It's coming along nicely, son. But you'll not get it finished today. We need to be heading soon. We daren't be late. You know what your mother's like.'

Why did they have to go to this evening Mass anyway? Mairead and her notions. Prayers for Peace are not going to put an end to the likes of Derek Dunne having to uproot his family.

A stiff slug of vodka brings him back to the present moment.

'I want to paint the birds,' Kieran is saying as he wipes the paint brush and reaches for the palette again.

It's his first attempt at oils. The results are impressive. Kieran is the most talented student Danny has come across in his twenty years of teaching.

'Well, we're leaving in fifteen minutes,' Paddy says, raising his eyebrows at Danny.

'Perhaps you need to work on the sky a fraction first, Kieran,' Danny says in his mellifluous Cork accent, pointing to certain parts of the canvas while explaining about light and texture.

Paddy floats on the periphery of their interaction, a fingertip caressing the groove running along the rim of his half-full glass. His back sinks further into the armchair and he half closes his eyes. There's a cosiness about this terraced house despite the layers of dust and blatant disorderliness. Danny Lynch is a loner and an eccentric, but he's a decent man. And he's the best arts and crafts teacher the town has seen.

'We can start on the birds next time,' Danny is saying. 'Work on your own now for a while and remember – light strokes.'

Kieran's gruff response tells Paddy he's disappointed. It's best to ignore him; placating never works. Paddy turns his attention to Danny who has sat down again.

'Did you see the news last night, Danny? Bernadette Devlin was released from prison.'

Danny leans forward. The truth is he's been overly engrossed in the lesson today. Usually he breaks it up with a bit of political banter and current affairs. There isn't much going on in the world that Danny Lynch doesn't have an opinion about.

'I did indeed hear that particular piece of news, Patrick,' he replies, placing his glass on the coffee table.

No one calls him Patrick. No one ever has, except his mother. But Danny refuses to abbreviate names.

'I'm a man of no denomination, as you well know, Patrick, but the politicians are positively preposterous if they view repression as a means of restoring order. Bernadette Devlin personifies all things democratic. She has courageously and unerringly stood up for the basic right of all nations to fight injustice.'

No one could put a sentence together better than Danny Lynch. Impeccable diction.

'So long as there are governments that strive to suppress the voice of the people, individuals – men and women like Martin Luther King and Bernadette Devlin – will stand up to them and lead by example, without fear of death.' Danny goes on, ready to plunge into his obsession with Martin Luther King. It seems the only subject he wants to discuss these days and he has an uncanny knack of being able to steer a conversation any which way. But while Paddy might admire Dr King, he doesn't share Danny's passion. He cuts in quick as lightning.

'So, where did you say you're heading tomorrow?'

It's a safe subject; Danny likes to talk about his meanderings.

'Letterkenny probably, though if the weather stays dry, I might wander on down to Ramelton,' he replies, getting up to refill his glass.

Danny is a lucky man, being able to hop on a bus at the drop of a hat and go wherever his fancy takes him. Paddy waits for him to sit down, but he doesn't. Instead, he goes to the window and stares out. His bulging Adam's apple moves rhythmically with each robotic sip, an Adam's apple that would be ugly on another man, but which goes well with Danny's lean, muscular torso. Paddy's gaze is fixed on this when he becomes aware that Danny is staring at him. Their eyes lock for a second. Paddy quickly downs the last of his vodka, then sets the empty glass on the table.

'Good God Almighty, the heat of that fire. We'd better be getting a move on,' he says, standing up. He has to steady himself, get his head to stop spinning. Bloody Hell. Danny Lynch knows how to pour a mean drink.

'Did you hear me, son? We need to be getting back.'

Kieran puts down the palette and lifts the stained cloth. His mood is getting worse.

'Will you be calling into Murphy's at all tomorrow evening? I'll be back around six.' Danny's voice is quiet, monotone.

'Oh, I doubt it. We're playing bridge.' Paddy's voice is way too loud. 'I might manage to squeeze a quick pint in if Leo lets us out on time.'

He lifts his jacket from the back of the settee and rummages in his pockets for the car key.

'Right, boyo, let's get this show on the road. We're cutting it a bit fine. Can't have Father Joe getting there before us, now can we?' Paddy jokes, holding up Kieran's coat.

Kieran grabs it and walks on ahead towards the front door. 'Not *we*. If Sinead's not going, I'm not going.'

'Try telling that to your mother, son.'

But Kieran has already shot outside and almost reached the car, parked on the other side of the street. If Paddy wasn't so worried about getting home quickly, he would put Kieran to shame for being so cheeky in front of Danny.

'Thanks for the lesson, Danny. He's coming on great. I think it's helping him a lot.'

'No need to be thanking me, Patrick.'

Danny's mood is subdued. He must get very lonely. He doesn't seem to have any other close friends – none that Paddy is aware of, anyhow. Paddy wouldn't have to leave if it wasn't for this stupid evening Mass. He'll know better than to listen to Mairead next time.

Oh, but of course! There's the talent competition Sinead is in later on tonight. He'd have had to leave anyway at some point. His head is definitely away with it. How could he have totally forgotten about the talent competition? They'd been rehearsing for weeks.

'I'll be seeing you then,' Paddy says, popping a Polo Mint into his mouth. 'Feels like there's a frost in the air,' he adds, pulling his lapels over his chest.

Danny has already gone back indoors by the time the car reverses out of the parking space. There was something Paddy had wanted to ask him. Danny usually waits at the door until the car pulls away. Anyway, maybe they'll get wrapped up sooner rather than later at the bookies tomorrow so he can drop into Murphy's for a quick one.

Kieran doesn't say a word the whole way home and Paddy makes no effort either.

When the car pulls up outside the house he keeps the engine running and the headlights on full. The Polo Mint has melted into a sliver and is jagging the sack of flesh under his tongue.

'Tell your mother to bring me my coat,' he calls after Kieran.

The slats on the venetian blinds in the front bedroom open and close in a flash, like a beacon light, a warning: Prepare for Battle. Paddy takes a fresh mint from the packet and pulls the car seat closer to the steering wheel.

'What kept you, Paddy? We'll be lucky to get a seat,' Mairead says, scowling and getting into the car. 'Niamh, hurry up and get in,' she snaps. 'Niall! Move over and stop that nonsense. We're late enough as it is. Paddy, you'll have to have a word with Kieran when we get back. He needs a good slap.'

Mairead's solution to everything – 'a good slap'.

As soon as they're settled, he edges the car from the kerb and heads up towards the top of the estate. No use asking where his coat is.

'Why don't you just reverse instead of going the whole way round the Green?'

'Mairead, will you take it easy, for the love of God. Have you ever known Father Joe to start a Mass on time?'

'That's not the point, Paddy,' she says.

She takes the handbag from the crook of her arm and places it on her lap, holding on tightly to the straps, and stares out the window.

Moan, moan, moan … does she never get tired of it? Despite himself, Paddy presses harder on the accelerator.

There are a few stragglers making their way towards the chapel door as he pulls up outside the gates to let Mairead and the children out. He'll have to go on further to find a parking spot. There's no rush. As long as he's there before the readings, he's covered. Come to think of it, would anyone even notice if he didn't go at all?

When he eventually enters the chapel, Father Joe and the altar boys have already taken up their positions but the organ is still playing. A few men are standing at the back. Surprisingly, the chapel is nearly full. He spots a place along the right-hand-side aisle and slips into the pew just as the opening prayer begins. He blesses himself before scanning the chapel in search of Mairead and the children. Niamh and Niall are four rows in front of him but there's no sign of Mairead. Just as they're about to sit down Niamh turns her head and he catches her eye. 'Where's Mammy?' he mouths, and she points across to the middle aisle where Mairead is sitting on the inside of Johnny Blee.

Is that a new hat she's wearing? He hadn't noticed it earlier.

Paddy shifts in his seat.

Either that sleazeball Blee came in after her and she moved over to make room, or he was there first and let her in, which meant she would have had to brush past him. Seeing they were so late in arriving, the latter scenario was the more likely of the two. You'd think she could have found a different spot. Paddy has seen Johnny Blee in action one time too many. How women can't see through him, good looks or no good looks, beats Paddy. Of course, it helps that he's got a few bob about him.

There's always a draught from the back of the church, even when the doors are closed, and wouldn't you know that Father Joe has decided to give a longer sermon than usual.

Paddy folds his arms and tucks his fists up close to his armpits. He stretches his neck right and left to release the stiffness and the cold that has crept in from the moment he got into the pew. Midway through the right stretch, he pauses to look up at the third station of the cross: Jesus falls the first time. His eyes flick to the fourth: Jesus meets his mother, Mary.

Mary, the mother of all mothers. You never see her smiling. Right enough, you wouldn't expect the woman to be smiling on the road to Calvary, but she always looks depressed in her pictures. There can't have been much joy knowing you'd have to sacrifice your only son.

The offertory is already in full swing by the time Paddy refocuses on the liturgy. He glances over at Mairead, whose head seems to be bent in prayer. Blee would do better to keep his eyes down if he knows what's good for him.

'… Hosanna in the highest. Blessed is he who comes in the name of the Lord. Hosanna in the highest …'

Blee has stepped out of the pew and is bending over to pick something up from under the seat in front. It's a hymn book. He wipes it clean with his sleeve and hands it to Mairead, whose profile is now in view. She hasn't a note in her head so she's no need for a hymn book but she's smiling in gratitude as she takes it from Blee.

'… Christ has died, Christ is risen, Christ will come again …'

Paddy hasn't fasted. He can't receive Holy Communion.

'… Lord, I am not worthy to receive you, but only say the word and I shall be healed …'

The organ starts up and the congregation file out of their pews to form the procession for Holy Communion. Niamh and Niall are first out and Mairead rises quickly. Johnny Blee stands to make room, but instead of simply getting out he forces her to brush past him once again. And Mairead has no sooner stepped in to the aisle than he's right behind her in the procession, the lecherous, heathenish hypocrite!

Paddy is out of his seat like a bullet and joins the line running parallel to Mairead's. People shouldn't have to fast before receiving communion. The Vatican would need to lighten up on some of these stupid rules.

He's only three heads behind and his line is moving faster. By the time he reaches Blee, his fingertips are sore from pressing into his knuckles. Blee would have to be stupid not to realise that Paddy was on to him.

Mairead hasn't noticed Paddy standing almost beside her now so he switches his eyes in the direction of the pulpit, adopting a trance-like expression. Then he turns his gaze towards the altar ahead of him in time to see Niamh and Niall take their places, ready to receive. He winks at the pair of them as they pass him on their way back and he moves forward to kneel at the altar. Mairead is behind him now.

'The Body of Christ,' says the assisting priest, a visiting curate.

'Amen.'

Paddy sticks out his tongue and drags the wafer in, pressing it against the roof of his mouth. He blesses himself and turns, just as Mairead and Blee are moving over to the left of the altar. By the time Paddy kneels in his pew, the wafer has melted into a soggy membrane that his tongue struggles to dislodge. He keeps his head bowed as if in prayer as Father Joe rattles on about parish business. For once, he manages to keep it brief. The congregation is standing.

'The Mass is ended. Go in peace to love and serve the Lord.'

Paddy is out of his pew the minute he spits out his 'Thanks be to God'.

There's a spot by the door. He'll wait for them all there.

Niamh and Niall are the first to appear.

'Daddy, don't forget you have to stop at the shop for our sweets.'

They pull at his jacket.

'I heard you. When have I ever forgotten your sweets?' he snaps, not looking at them. His gaze is fixed on Mairead. She is engrossed in something Johnny Blee is telling her.

'There's your mother. Come on, let's go,' he says, pushing the children towards the point where their paths will meet.

'Paddy, did you know that Mrs Blee passed away last week?' Mairead says the minute she reaches Paddy.

No, he hadn't known Johnny's mother had died.

'Sorry for your loss, Johnny,' Paddy says, eyeballing Blee.

'Thanks, Paddy. Ach, sure it was probably for the best. She'd been poorly for years.'

And she must have been a hundred if she was a day, Blee, so stop acting like your world's been turned upside down just to get tea and sympathy from my wife.

It has started to rain.

'We're parked further up so we'll have to make a dash for it,' Paddy says. He pulls his jacket collar up round his neck.

'Johnny, do you need a lift?' Mairead offers, stepping into the first drops of rain.

'Well, I came on foot but sure I'm only five minutes up the road.'

'Not at all, you'll get soaked. There's plenty of room in the car. We have to stop at the shop anyway, isn't that right, Paddy?'

They always stop at Brown's Confectionery when they go to chapel on the other side of town. And, of course, Johnny Blee would happen to live only two doors further down.

When they've all piled into the car, with Johnny in the front seat, Paddy starts the engine and waits for it to warm up. The rain is belting down now. Johnny makes small talk with Niamh and Niall, feigning interest in what they want to be when they grow up. How else can the bastard get a legitimate eyeful of Mairead? He must think Paddy was born yesterday. And Mairead can't be that stupid. Does she not see that she's encouraging him?

They pull up near the shop. Paddy and Johnny get out of the car simultaneously.

'Here, Mairead, do you want to get into the front?' Johnny asks, flipping the back of the front seat forward to let her out.

'Thanks, Johnny,' she says, taking his outstretched hand.

'God Bless, and tell your mother my aunty Nuala was asking for her,' he says, closing the car door.

Yeah, yeah, Johnny. Pull the other one, would you. When was the last time your aunty Nuala and Mairead's mother clapped eyes on each other?

'I'll see you around, Paddy. Thanks for the lift.' Johnny is almost at his front door before Paddy can reply.

'Yes, see you around.'

The shop is busy. It's always the way of things after evening Mass. Paddy lifts a paper bag and counts four Drumsticks and four packets of Parma Violets for Kieran, Sinead, Niamh and Niall. The wee ones will already be in bed. His head is throbbing and his mouth is parched. He reaches for a bottle of Lucozade and downs it in two gulps.

'Sorry, Eugene, I couldn't wait,' he says, handing over the empty bottle and the sweets to Eugene Gallagher.

'Aw now, Master Reilly, I'll have to charge you a wee bit extra for that one,' Eugene jokes.

Normally Paddy would keep the banter going. Eugene Gallagher was one of the pupils in the first classroom he stepped into as a fully qualified teacher. Not much grey matter but a great footballer. 'Master Reilly' has stuck, and it never fails to stir a smile in Paddy each time he hears it being used by these grown men. But on this occasion a fake smile is the best he can muster as he hands over the money and heads back to the car.

'What did you think of the sermon?' Mairead asks after a minute of silent driving.

'Didn't pay too much attention to it,' Paddy replies dryly.

'Actually, I thought it was one of his better sermons,' Mairead goes on.

Another minute of silence.

'Father Joe is getting a bit senile though. I mean, it's time he retired,' she tries again.

Why is she acting as if nothing is wrong? She knows damn well I'm in no mood for inconsequential chit-chat.

'They say that young curate will go places. He has a lovely speaking voice. I'd say most of the congregation actually listened to the readings this evening.'

More stonewalling.

She gets the message.

He parks the car, turns off the engine, slams the car door and is halfway up the front path before she manages to get the children out of the car.

'Paddy,' Mairead calls after him. 'Are you not going to lock the car?'

The children have caught up with him.

'Daddy, Mammy's calling you.' Niall and Niamh scoot inside before him.

'Paddy!'

He ignores her and walks on into the living room, leaving the front door ajar behind him. Sinead is in the kitchen.

Kieran must be upstairs. He puts the bag of sweets on the mantelpiece, lifts *The Irish News* lying on the couch and sits down on the armchair nearest the fire.

Enough is enough. He's sick and tired of being taken for a fool. He's not going to let her or anyone else walk all over him like this. Not any more.

II. Sinead

Daddy might be in the doghouse and trying to be on his best behaviour, but this carry-on with the spinach isn't funny any more. I didn't think it was that hilarious the first time, even if I did happen to laugh a bit with the rest of them. I don't get why he doesn't stop it.

'Daddy, he's going to be sick, so he is.'

Eamon is gagging again. The wee ones and Niamh are giggling themselves silly.

'Ach Sinead, would you relax,' Daddy says.

He can smile all he likes but he knows I'm right.

'Here, son, do you want to spit it out?'

He's taking the tin of disgusting spinach out of Eamon's hand. But wouldn't you know? Eamon shakes his head and does a Popeye move with his muscles. That's the thing … he actually believes spinach can turn him into Muscle Man.

They're all in hysterics again, even Daddy.

Okay, I'll admit it was funny when Eamon ate a whole

half tin the first time. Especially when he started puffing out his chest like Tarzan and getting us all to feel how hard the muscles on the tops of his arms and legs were. He went around for days like Popeye, convinced he had developed superpowers. But there's no way that's going to happen again. He's only on his second spoonful and he can't swallow the stuff.

I've had enough. I'm going upstairs … as a protest. It's what Bernadette Devlin would do if she were me. When I grow up, I want to be like Bernadette Devlin. Daddy says she's so clever she could buy and sell the whole British government. I'm not sure if I should make some sort of a speech before I go just so Daddy knows I'm leaving in protest but I'll bang the door a bit – though not so much that he might think it's not a peaceful protest. Daddy says everyone should fight for their rights so long as they don't 'resort to violence'.

But I don't even get as far as the door when Eamon starts choking.

'You see, you see? I told you!' I'm shouting at Daddy.

No one's laughing now. There's spinach puke all over the lino. Serves Daddy right. He's already in trouble with Mammy and this isn't going to help him.

'Sinead, quick, tell your mother to give you a cloth and a basin of water.'

Tell your mother, tell your father, tell your mother, tell your father … I'm sick of it. Mammy's already filling the basin in the kitchen when I go in. This time two weeks things will be back to normal.

I keep repeating this in my head and my tummy settles down. I always get the vomity feeling when they're not talking to each other. I used to say 'this time next week' because the huffing never used to last long. But recently I've changed it to two weeks just to be sure. The thing is, if Mammy wasn't so stubborn, it would probably be over far quicker. Daddy's the one who always ends up trying his best to be friendly after a few days have passed but she doesn't take him on, which then makes him stubborn and the two of them act like a couple of wains. I mean, not even me and Niamh fall out for more than two days and Niamh takes the biscuit when it comes to stubbornness. She's more like Mammy in that department. I take after Daddy.

Actually, I've just realised I'm saying 'this time two weeks' over and over in my head when more than a week has already passed. This time next week, this time next week – I don't want to jinx things.

'Tell Eamon to come here and get his face washed,' Mammy says, throwing a cloth into the suds and handing me the basin.

Go flamin' tell him yourself.

'Eamon, Mammy says to go get your face scrubbed.'

Daddy takes the basin from me and puts it on the floor near the goo. At least he doesn't expect me to wipe it up. He's still in good form though.

'I think your muscles have had enough spinach for a while. Even Popeye can get a sickener of it.'

Daddy feels sorry for Eamon now but he's trying to hide it. Well, I hope he feels bad. He goes on too much about Eamon being a stick. He might say it as a joke but he's always comparing him to Michael, who looks the same age. Of course, Michael is going to be the next Bobby Charlton, according to Daddy. So what if Eamon is too skinny and has no talent? What about Kieran? He might play football but he's useless – two left feet. I never hear Daddy pulling his leg. Mind you, Kieran wouldn't see the joke, knowing Kieran, whereas Eamon giggles as much as the rest of us when Daddy says things like 'It's the ball you're meant to kick, son, not the turf.'

And now Daddy is handing me the dirty basin to bring back into the kitchen.

'Why can't Niamh take it in?'

'No way,' shouts Niamh and runs for upstairs before Daddy can change his mind.

I reach for the basin and give it to Mammy, who's standing at the scullery sink where she has finished wiping Eamon's face.

'Someone has to dig up some potatoes for dinner,' she tells me. I know she really means Kieran should do it.

There's going to be a fight. No one likes having to fill the bucket with potatoes. It was Daddy's bright idea to sow part of the garden, but we end up having to dig forever to fill a measly bucket because half of them are rotten. And whoever is doing the digging has to feel each potato to see if it's okay. Half the time we have to scrape off gigantic lumps of hard clay only to discover a spud the size of a pea underneath. Daddy won't admit that it was a stupid idea and he's forever complimenting Mammy's dinners so that he can get it in about the potatoes.

'That meat's cooked to a tee, Mairead, and the potatoes are like balls of flour.'

There's another thing – why do adults go on so much about boiled potatoes being like 'balls of flour' as if it's a big deal? I mean, they're dry and tasteless and crumble to pieces when you stick a fork in them. I have to mash them up and mix them with gravy, and even then I can't eat them. I've learnt a good trick to fool Mammy into thinking I've eaten my dinner. I mash and spread the spuds to the edge of the plate so that there's a big, empty hole in the middle, where I place my knife and fork.

'One of yous has to fill the bucket with potatoes,' I announce.

'What do you mean "one of yous"? What are those things dangling on the end of your arms, Sinead?' Kieran says, poking his head over the top of the couch where he's been lying like a corpse the whole time.

'Actually, it's your turn, smart alec. And anyway, I didn't see you jumping up to help with the basin.'

'Stop fighting, the pair of you. I'll do it myself,' Daddy says.

It would be a very different story if Daddy wasn't trying to get on Mammy's good side. Kieran's jammy like that. He always gets out of having to do things. But I suppose anything Daddy can do to get Mammy to soften up is good. Then we can get back to normal.

I still don't understand what happened this time, but it all started when they came back in after Mass last Friday evening. I got out of going because I had to look after the wee ones. When I asked Niamh later what had happened, she said she didn't know. Daddy went to the shop to buy our sweets, that's all. Then one minute Mammy was talking and the next thing Niamh knew, Daddy was marching into the house. As for Niall, he hadn't noticed anything was wrong. But then he wouldn't because he's always on cloud nine, dreaming about becoming a film director or an actor, or both.

It took me a few minutes to notice that something was wrong because I was dying to show Mammy her surprise. I'd put the three wee ones to bed like I was told, but I'd also cleared up the kitchen and made supper without being asked. And apart from wanting to show her the surprise, I was also excited about taking part in the first round of the talent competition that night at nine o'clock.

Me and my friend Claire Donoghue had been practising our song all week with Daddy: 'The Bold Gendarmes'.

I didn't like the song at all. I wanted to sing 'The Green, Green Grass of Home'. But Daddy said 'The Bold Gendarmes' was the perfect song for a talent contest. And he would know – he's been an adjudicator at a whole pile of talent competitions. We had to sing and march, and we even had officers' hats to lift up and down, like the Black and White Minstrels.

Now, I don't want to sound as if I'm bumming my own load but I was really good at the moves, unlike Claire, who we soon discovered doesn't know what the word 'rhythm' means. Her legs would fly off in the opposite direction to mine and in slow motion. In the end, we had to change the rhythm of the song to fit her legs but even then she couldn't get it right.

'They'll not be calling you the Bold Gendarmes after that nifty performance, Sinead. More like the Fool Gendarmes.'

Kieran was banned from the living room during rehearsals after that helpful comment. And he got a proper telling off for being nasty and making me lose my confidence. Daddy had been telling me all week not to worry about it, that it was 'the singing that counts', and I'd managed to put thoughts of looking like an eejit out of my head.

So anyway, last Friday evening, with all this going through my head, Daddy had sat down in the armchair with a big face on him and was staring into the newspaper before

I understood that something was wrong. The brown paper bag with our sweets was on the mantelpiece.

'I did the dishes and made sandwiches and tea,' I said, looking at Mammy.

'Good girl yourself, Sinead,' she said, taking her coat off.

'What kind of sandwiches did you make?' Niall piped in. 'I'm starving.'

Of course, he started moaning because he hates tinned salmon, so I told him I'd make him one with cheese – anything to stop him complaining and making things worse because by then Mammy's forehead was puckered up and her mouth was like Granny Boyle's when she forgets to put her teeth in.

'What's the matter with you, Paddy?' she scolded, impatiently lifting the poker to stoke the fire, which didn't need stoking.

Well, I don't know what got into Daddy. Anyone would have thought he had gone bonkers. He jumped up off the chair with a face the colour of beetroot and went right up close to Mammy, who was taking two steps back. The poker was still in her hand and her mouth was hanging open in pure shock.

'Are you going to have the audacity to stand there and pretend you don't know exactly what this is about? Do you really take me for an imbecile?' he shouted, like he was going to burst a blood vessel.

'Would you please sit down – and don't dare talk to me like that,' Mammy said, in as calm a voice as she could. But her hand was shaking when she set the poker against the wall near the fire. 'For your information, I haven't a clue what you're going on about.'

But Daddy didn't sit down. He turned his back on her

and was heading for the door when Mammy, being stupid, called after him, 'You're a bloody nutter, that's what you are.'

What did she have to go and say that for?

She'd lifted the nearest cushion and was punching it into shape, which meant she wasn't scared any more. Just angry. It's one of the things Mammy does when she's losing her temper. Daddy is completely different. When he's in bad form he usually just goes quiet. He hardly ever loses his temper. Which is why I was as shocked as Mammy with the way he was acting.

Of course, the minute Mammy called him a 'nutter' my heart started pounding. Suddenly, he stopped in his tracks, turned around in a flash, and when he saw Mammy wasn't taking him on, he grabbed the bag of sweets and hurled them on the floor in front of the fireplace. That got Mammy to look at him quick enough. And wouldn't you know that Drama Queen Niamh would let a scream out of her, which got Daddy's attention but didn't help things one bit – it just made him angrier with Mammy.

'Are you happy now, Mairead?' he shouted, going over to Niamh. 'Shush, pet, we'll get more tomorrow. Sinead, I'm sorry but there will be no talent contest tonight. You have your mother to thank for that one,' he said, lifting his coat off the chair.

The next thing I knew he was out the door and getting into the car. I couldn't believe my ears – after all our practising! But then, I suppose, I probably wouldn't have enjoyed it anyway, which is why I couldn't even feel angry. It wouldn't have been the same after what had happened.

My eyes were stinging though.

Kieran was upstairs, so me, Niamh and Niall started

picking the Parma Violets off the floor. We'd still be able to eat them, even the ones that had rolled under the couch. A bit of fluff never killed anyone. And the Drumsticks were fine. Only one got broke.

Mammy brought us out the salmon sandwiches and tea but went back into the kitchen without a word. We sat there looking at my lovely, triangle sandwiches with the crusts cut off, but obviously none of us was hungry. So I took the torn sweet bag and stuffed a handful of sandwiches into it, rolling the paper round and squashing them. Then I tucked the parcel in the waist band of my skirt, which was well hidden under my baggy jumper.

'Eat at least one,' I whispered to Niamh and Niall, lifting one of the sandwiches I'd left on the plate. I started mine but only managed a couple of bites. We drank down all our tea though, so I knew Mammy would be fine. And anyway, Kieran still had to eat his share. Niamh and Niall brought the things back into the kitchen and I scooted down to tell Claire we wouldn't be going. I stuffed the bag of sandwiches into Donoghue's hedge on the way. I still wanted to cry.

When I came back, Niamh and Niall had already started on their sweets but I couldn't eat mine so I put them upstairs under my pillow for later on.

That was over a week ago. And although Daddy disappeared for a couple of days, probably because he was still angry and wanted to calm down a bit, he's been here practically all the time these last five days, so it's obvious he's back to his usual, calm self. But there's no use trying to explain that to Mammy. That's what I mean when I say she's stubborn.

I've decided to go outside to where Daddy's digging the potatoes. I feel sorry for him because it's starting to rain.

Mammy is standing at the sink washing out the dirty cloth, and the stinky tin of spinach is sitting on the draining board. I've taken my wellies from the cubbyhole in the back hall and I'm squeezing my feet into them.

'If you're going outside, Sinead, dump that spinach in the big bin for me please,' Mammy says.

'Why do I have to do all the dirty work?' I say, taking it from her.

She smiles at me and I'm planning not to smile back, but then I change my mind.

'Yuck!' I say, but my voice is all jokey.

'Ach, you'll be all right,' she says, fixing my fringe a bit. 'And tell Daddy half a bucket is plenty.'

FEBRUARY
1971

I. Paddy

Riordan Duffy is by no means a stupid man but he lacks tact and has a way with words that can pound his listeners into silence. He wastes no time getting to the point after Paddy explains why he has called up to see him. Not that there was a need to explain anything. Riordan Duffy knows everything about everyone in the town, especially the families living on the estate. Riordan is a fast speaker and a loud speaker, and this rhetorical monologue, which is wrapped up in a lecture on the political history of Ireland, is beginning to grate on Paddy. Under the circumstances, though, he has no choice but to be patient. He grabs an opening when Riordan has to stop to light a cigarette.

'Riordan, I'm not for a second trying to say that the IRA doesn't have a point, but my niece is only eighteen years old and—'

'Look, Paddy,' Riordan interrupts, vigorously puffing as the match refuses to ignite the cigarette. 'We've beaten the life out of this. I'm only repeating myself.' He strikes another match. 'Your niece was given fair warning and if she'd done as she should have, she wouldn't be in this predicament. That baby is not going to protect her from a tarring and feathering after it's born.' Riordan almost pauses before delivering the next sentence. 'They're not monsters, Paddy. They're fighting a fucking war. And anyone consorting with the enemy is a traitor in the eyes of the Provisional Irish Republican Army – no exceptions. I'm not active but I know the rules. My advice to you, since that's what you're asking for, is to get her out of the country.'

Paddy fixes his gaze more intently on Riordan Duffy's insentient face. Riordan might be a staunch Republican, and done time because of it, but Paddy would never have labelled him a 'hard man'. He was as decent as the next fella. Hadn't they grown up in the same part of town, shared the same fanaticism for Celtic, played football and snooker with the gang?

Snooker balls.

Paddy lowers his eyes, tries to squeeze that memory of the snooker hall from his consciousness … his mother standing outside, calling his name … him trying to joke it off, cheeks blazing … Riordan Duffy and the rest of them staring.

Riordan's voice has become a distant drone.

Paddy presses the tips of his fingers hard against his temple to deflect the onslaught of memories the snooker hall scene is triggering: the weeks pleading with his mother, his father's passivity, the anger, the alienation, the relentless loneliness that had consumed him when he was forced to do his final year as a boarder at St Columb's. And the guilt, the enduring guilt, about the money borrowed to pay for his lazy, selfish behaviour.

He lifts his eyes. But sure hadn't it all been worth it, as Eileen was so fond of telling the whole world. Didn't he knuckle down, improve his grades, get into teaching college – end of story, everyone as happy as good old Larry.

He sits up straighter and refocuses. Weaving his fingers into a firm, prayer-like grip, he places his hands in his lap and nods intermittently as Riordan recounts some of the recent injustices Catholic civilians have suffered at the hands of the British army. Paddy braces himself, ready to step out of character. It's a trick he learned early in life, pretending to be someone else. As long as you don't get carried away with yourself there's no harm in it. He'll have to up the volume in his vocal chords.

'Riordan, we go back a long way,' he says, with a feigned fervour. 'You know me, you know my family, so you know we're devout Catholics. Yes, I agree, things have escalated and the British government has botched things—'

Riordan goes to speak but Paddy's determined. He even manages to go one notch louder.

'I get where you're coming from,' he continues, 'but the soldier is only nineteen years old – his mother's half Irish for God's sake. And my niece ended it, she ended it, Riordan. But she didn't know she was expecting. I mean, think about it – what did that young fella or my niece know when they shipped him over here? Weren't we all on the streets serving him and the rest of the feckin' British army tea and biscuits?'

Feckin' – a lame, girlie imitation of a profanity but the closest Paddy can bring himself to rough talk. And on and on he goes, like a broken record as if by pure force of repetition something might shift and Riordan will throw him a lifeline, try to use the influence he's pretending he doesn't have.

But the conversation ends abruptly when Riordan rises from the table.

Paddy pushes himself out of the chair and into silence. Only then does he notice the chaos that is the Duffys' living room: a sleeveless LP on the floor heavily flecked with dust, toy soldiers toppled amidst crumbs strewn over a threadbare sofa, an overflowing ashtray by the hearth, and a jaundiced, milky membrane floating on the cold remains of two half-full mugs of tea.

Still, despite the mess and the distinct odour, the house has a homely feel about it. 'A bit of dirt doesn't kill anyone', as Paddy's father would say when he was scolded for not taking off his work boots. His father would say a lot of ineffectual things.

Riordan is moving towards the front of the house. Paddy puts his coat back on and follows him.

'I can't help you, Paddy. Get the girl out of the country, have the baby, and give it up for adoption,' Riordan says, not for the first time that morning. He has his back to Paddy as he speaks. 'I've no inside information as such, but I'd say if she comes home, there's no guarantee she won't have to face a deferred punishment.'

Paddy nods, a fake show of understanding. There's nothing about any of this that he understands. Accepting is not synonymous with understanding.

'I'll pass it on to the family,' he says, trying to modify his voice in preparation for his next line of questioning. He can't go back home without at least trying to broach the other subject. Mairead will go berserk. And Paddy would rather keep the peace, especially after the last big row they had. The silent treatment had gone on for too long; the atmosphere had been unbearable. She'd even threatened to leave him, which is typical, hysterical Mairead. Okay, so her bark might be worse than her bite, as the saying goes, but still – it's hard to stomach at times. No wonder he takes himself off for a couple of days. Then when he's calmed down he's ready to forget about it. Unfortunately, though, it takes Mairead a lot longer to forgive and forget. Why the need for the long drawn-out antagonism? And now, just when things are fine between them, she's getting more and more uptight about this 'friendship' she insists Kieran has developed with Riordan's sons. For Pete's sake! How in God's name is he supposed to talk to Riordan about Mairead's ridiculous fears without sounding offensive?

He clears his throat of imaginary phlegm just as Riordan opens the lock on the front door.

'I've heard there are a lot of young ones signing up for the Youth Division. Wasn't that boy who got shot in the crossfire only thirteen?' Paddy asks, standing in the hallway. He fumbles with the buttons on his coat, avoiding eye contact.

'Aye, that's all he was, fucking bastards,' Riordan comes back at him.

Paddy's stomach lurches at the sudden vehemence.

Riordan has now reassumed the stance of an orator, denouncing 'the bloody British Empire and their propaganda'. For a man who only managed to scrape through primary school, he can fairly get his tongue around lengthy, highfalutin sentences. It would be stupid, potentially dangerous, in fact, for Paddy to say what's on his mind – actually, Mairead's paranoid mind. Let her come up here and tackle the subject with Riordan Duffy herself. She needs to get a grip on reality before she does everyone's head in.

Paddy finally steps out of the house and turns on the doorstep. Riordan has stirred in him a curious mix of horror, respect and envy. There is something disturbingly honourable about the fact that this man has lived his life by his convictions. The handshake is firm, resolute. Neither of them is happy with the outcome but they respect their differences.

Paddy heads back down the estate. He could postpone calling at Eileen's, go home first, have a bite to eat. But what's the point? Better get it over and done with. Besides, he'd only be swapping one unpleasant conversation for another. He still has to face Mairead and her questions.

Eileen and Gerard are sitting at opposite sides of the fireplace when Paddy enters their living room. The normally lively atmosphere in Eileen's home has been replaced by one more common at wakes.

'Where's Geraldine?' Paddy asks, closing the door quietly behind him.

'She's upstairs in her room. She won't come down.' Eileen's voice is listless.

Gerard glances at Paddy for a second before hanging his head in that defeatist way he has when the going gets tough. Gerard Donnelly should have been the one up there thrashing it out with the IRA, fighting for his daughter. But that option had never been on the table. As usual, it was up to Paddy to sort it out.

Eileen goes to lift herself out of her armchair to make Paddy a cup of tea but he signals for her to stay put. It'll soon be lunchtime. The visit to Riordan hadn't taken as long as he'd thought it would; he plans to work the half day, so he needs to be getting a move on.

Neither of them look at Paddy as they listen to the details

of his meeting with Riordan. Eileen is staring hypnotically at the blue flames struggling between newly mounted pieces of coal. Gerard's long, lean frame remains slouched in the armchair.

'It could be worse you know, Eileen,' and Paddy tells her about Mairead's brother in Manchester who can put Geraldine up until the baby is born.

But what's the point in talking on? He'll come back after work. Maybe they'll have got over the initial shock by then. And Geraldine might land down at any minute. Paddy can't face her. Gerard Donnelly can take over from here. Besides, Eileen is about to crack and raw emotion is not Paddy's thing – the comforting embrace that is expected of him stays trapped in his awkward arms.

'I'd better get going, but I'll call in later if you like,' he says.

His hand is already on the door handle. Eileen doesn't stand to see him out as she would normally do. Neither does Gerard. No surprises there. A combination of relief and sadness follows Paddy out the front door.

Crossing the Green towards the house, Niamh, who has been playing there, make a dash for him and he stops to catch her in his arms.

His princess.

For some reason, Niamh always reminds him of the Ugly Duckling story and he tends to give her more attention than the rest, which causes a bit of jealousy. When he carries her upstairs at bedtime like she's Sleeping Beauty, Sinead's jibes of 'big baby' fail to mask her annoyance, but he ignores it. Niamh's vulnerability is like a magnet, attracting bullies and cruelty. Even Sinead takes advantage of her. One day, the thick glasses will be gone, along with the gawkiness, and

Niamh will learn to stand her ground. Until then, he is her knight in shining armour.

As he sets her back down on the grass, Paddy glances over at Sinead who is sitting on the kerb outside the house. She looks down in the dumps. God knows he's had enough misery for one day, and yet by the time he reaches the footpath, a slight swing in his mood draws a joke from him as he passes Sinead. Not that it achieves anything. Nothing to do but let her wallow in it. He goes on into the house.

'What's up with Sinead? The face on her out there would put the wind up a banshee,' Paddy calls out to Mairead who's washing dishes in the scullery.

He's taking off his coat when she walks into the living room, drying her hands on a tea towel.

'Oh, you're back. I wasn't expecting you for a while. Well? How did it go? Not good, from the look on your face,' Mairead says. She places the towel over the arm of the chair and sits down.

No way is he for going over the whole thing again.

'I'll fill you in later because I'm going to head on down to the bookies, but in a nutshell – she has to get out of Ireland.'

Mairead is silent. She lifts the tea towel and folds it before laying it on her knee and smoothing it down. It's obvious she wants to ask about Kieran but is waiting for him to volunteer information. Well, that's not going to happen. Paddy heads towards the scullery but steals a sideway glance en route.

'I thought you said you weren't working this weekend?' she says, her eyes drilling into his spine.

'I know, but no point in missing half a day's pay, is there?'

He's opened the fridge and is peering into it. Her eyes are still there, closer. Will she or won't she? Please, please, don't ask about Kieran. He's banking on the seriousness of Geraldine's situation. It would be in bad taste to focus attention on Kieran.

Now she's moving away from him, putting the tea towel on its hook. She tells him she has to go into town for an hour to get the messages. She's taking Sinead with her.

So Kieran is not on her mind at all?

He follows her back into the living room where she's focusing her attention on stoking the fire. Her face is sad, a sadness that has got nothing to do with him.

'The scuttle needs refilling,' she says, straightening her back. 'Get Kieran to do it.'

Maybe Kieran is on her mind after all.

Her sombre tone is unnerving. Does he want to know what's wrong? No, he's got enough on his mind. Does she even want to talk about it? No, probably not. She would have said something by now.

'Go you on and get ready. I'll hold the fort. I don't know if I can face the bookies today anyway,' he says, trying to sound upbeat. His own melancholy is a scab he's been scratching for days. 'What will I make them for lunch? They'll be coming in soon, starving,' he adds, walking back to the scullery.

Whatever it is she's mulling over he's not the one to help her with it. Not today. He doesn't want to talk any more. He shouldn't have to. She shouldn't expect him to. She should know how tough a day it has been. Mairead doesn't know what problems are.

What's keeping her? Why doesn't she just go on upstairs and get ready?

He fills the kettle and immerses himself in domestic activity, rattling saucepans as he searches in the cupboard for the frying pan. He is faint with hunger and the bacon he's spotted at the back of the fridge has sent his taste buds into a frenzy. He's got time to make himself a bacon butty before Mairead leaves. That way he'll be free to keep an eye on the brood while she's gone. Images of knobs of melting butter on toast and HP Sauce tease him as he reaches into the fridge for the lard and packet of bacon. He places them on the workbench.

'Have you decided what they're going to eat?' he calls out.

'Just make them beans on toast. We won't be that long anyway. Shauna's not due a feed yet. She might be ready for a nap soon,' Mairead calls back, still hesitating.

What's wrong with her? But a few seconds later there is the creak of the stairs being mounted and the coast is finally clear. He strips off four slices of streaky bacon and slaps them onto the knob of melting lard in the frying pan. Then he aligns them carefully with a fork so that each slice will brown evenly. The sparks of sizzling fat on his hand force him to lift the pan off the cooker while he lowers the gas flame. Placing the pan back on the ring, he carefully flips the slices over and tries to get images of Geraldine and the hunched up figure of Sinead out of his head.

II. SINEAD

MY BUM'S FREEZING. I shouldn't have to sit on the bloody kerb. I'm sick of Mammy going on and on at me.

Sinead, would you stop this moping about. Out you go and get some fresh air.

And I'm sick of Daddy's jokes.

Sinead, would you pick your jaws up off that kerb!

Though I'd rather have Daddy's stupid jokes than have to listen to Mammy going on all the time about me having to grow up and 'get my head out of the clouds'. What if I don't want to grow up? So what if I'm 'the only first year in the grammar school who believes in Santa Claus'?

I don't care about Santa Claus any more and of course I don't want to believe in him. But that's not the point. The point is I didn't like being handed a pound note to go and get whatever I wanted in Woolworths. I ended up buying a stupid brown, suede shoulder bag because Mammy said I might be getting too old for toys. I didn't want a toy. But

I didn't want a flamin' shoulder bag either. If it was up to Daddy, we'd believe in Santa Claus for as long as we liked. Which is a bit stupid. But that's not the point either. I hate Christmas now anyway. The real point here is I don't see why I can't lie on the couch all day and pretend to read or watch TV if I want. It's no skin off Mammy's nose, is it? Well, she might be able to force me to go outside, but she can't make me do anything else. And she can't make me tell her why I'm in such a bad mood.

The truth is it's more than just a bad mood. I can't describe the feeling. It's like sometimes I'm standing outside my own body and I'm two different people. The one walking around looks like me, talks like me, but isn't me. It must be the way robots feel. The other one, the invisible one, isn't like me either because all she wants to do is smash things or cry. She hears voices too and they don't always have friendly things to say. Sometimes the invisible me settles down and joins the robot me. But then I'm just a misery guts and that's when people won't leave me alone.

You see? How am I to explain all that to Mammy? Even if I wanted to tell her, she wouldn't understand. She'd think I'm bonkers, ready for the loony bin. So what's the point? I've never felt this way ever before, so it has to have something to do with the Calling.

Oh, I just wish I knew for sure what God wants. I bet Father Logue would know if I told him about the signs. I wish we had priests like him here. That day at the school retreat was brilliant (the only good thing about going to the grammar school) and Father Logue must be the funniest, handsomest priest in the whole of Ireland. He isn't stuck up, like the ones in our parish. He called me a 'beautiful Irish colleen' when I was rushing down the corridor on my own to go to the loo. I'd sneaked out of Father Quinn's morning Mass and Sister flamin' Alphonsus had given me a dirty look so I wanted to get back quickly. Why do nuns have to have men's names? Anyway, when I saw Father Logue coming in my direction, I slowed down. I wasn't going to be rude now, was I? Of course, I stood like a nincompoop with beetroot cheeks and not a word to say. But Father Logue is so friendly. He put his arm around my shoulder and asked me how I was doing. I couldn't look at him because he's the spit of Paul Newman and I go all wobbly just thinking about Paul Newman. When I said everything was brilliant, he put both his arms around me, dead tight, and kissed the top of my head before telling me I'd better hurry or they would be sending a search party out for me. I couldn't wait to tell Deirdre Malloy and Roisin Ramsay.

If I hadn't met Father Logue, I wouldn't have found out about the Calling so soon. I'd never heard of it before. Most of the girls in my class had gone to the convent primary school so it was no news to them. But at Daddy's school, we didn't have many Religion lessons. Daddy says you can't learn how to be a good Christian out of a book and we had more important things to do. We only did a bit of Religion when the Inspector was coming.

When I got back from the retreat, I was on cloud nine. It was a weird kind of feeling, all peaceful and serene like you were supposed to feel before you got the Calling – well, according to the nuns and priests, and they should know. So all I had to do was wait for the signs. And sure enough they started to come almost right away.

The first one came when me and Niamh were walking home from Mass. We had three new pence between us to get something in the shop. Niamh wanted a Curly Wurly to share. Normally, I would tell her where to go because I'm not fussed about Curly Wurlys. But guess what? Yep, I let her have it and I only took one small bite.

There were other small signs too. I did the dishes and generally helped Mammy without being asked. I let Eamon and Michael beat me at Ludo. I let Orla Gray copy my English comprehension answers and even helped her to write them a bit differently so Sister Aloysius wouldn't catch on. There were lots of little signs like these. But the most important sign came when our new Freeman's catalogue was delivered. After that, I was absolutely sure I had the Calling.

The thing is, usually I'd be dying to get a look at all the new pictures in the underwear section but this time I didn't blink an eyelid. This was the most important sign because, for ages, I couldn't stop myself from … anyway the point is it's a very bad habit that I knew I had to stop. Plus I was feeling guilty that I couldn't go to confession any more. It was far too embarrassing. Father Duncan must be the nosiest priest on earth, wanting me to explain my sins in detail. I just couldn't go back and it had been five weeks since my last confession.

Sure, doesn't God know the details? Isn't he 'omnipresent'? And God can figure out if you're sorry or not without you having to get in a confessional box with an old fogey like Father Duncan. Of course, Mammy wouldn't agree with me on that one. She would have a fit if she found out I'd stopped going. Though you don't really mind having to go to confession if you haven't committed any serious sins, do you?

That's why it was a brilliant feeling when I stopped my bad habit. I had even decided to send a letter to Father Logue and I was planning to tell Mammy and Daddy about the Calling after the school closed for the Easter holidays. Maybe they would agree to drive down to have a chat with Father Logue and get some advice. But everything started to go wrong one week after the retreat.

Niamh and I had a huge fight (which she started) and Daddy blamed me for the whole thing. I was so angry that I ran outside and sat by myself on the bench at the top end of the Green. I would have been fine but our Kieran passed by and called me 'Mopey Dick' in front of everyone. Then he called me a few other things when I called him 'a freak'. I could see he took it the wrong way and thought I was making fun of his petit mal. But I wouldn't do that, never in a million years. I knew he'd never believe me and that started my bad mood. And the next two days it got worse. By Wednesday, I couldn't stop myself from opening the Freeman's catalogue.

I understand that 'God works in mysterious ways', as Granny was forever telling us, and maybe he was only testing me, but there have been no more signs and I'm back to where I was and maybe worse. I dreamt last night that Father Logue asked me to marry him and kissed me. Okay, when I say me, it wasn't actually me as I am now. I didn't look like me in the dream. I looked like Liesl in *The Sound of Music*, with blonde hair and all. But who dreams of marrying a priest? It's awful.

So I'm not sure now if I've had the Calling or not. But I want to have it more than anything in the world. I don't want to marry anyone else except God, especially not if what Kieran says is true about how babies are made. And it must be true because Geraldine Donnelly isn't married to that British soldier and I thought you could only have babies if you were married. I'm not supposed to know, but it isn't my fault Mammy and Daddy can't keep their voices down when they're talking in the morning. Knowing Mammy, she'd probably think I was eavesdropping.

Everything is a mess, and Mammy is just making things worse by going on and on about me moping about. Why can't people just leave other people alone? I wish it would start raining and I wouldn't have to sit on this crappy kerb watching Niamh trying to play crappy cricket. She's useless.

I'm just thinking of going back inside to tell Mammy I've homework to do for Monday when suddenly she appears out of nowhere like Endora from *Bewitched*. She has her coat and hat on and is holding the brown patent bag Aunty Moira gave her for Christmas.

'Come on, Sinead, you and I are going for a wee run into town,' she says.

'What?'

'I have to get the groceries and you can help me carry them to the car. Then we can go to McNamee's for a pastry and a cup of tea,' she says.

'O-kaaay,' I say.

Weird. The last time me and Mammy went to McNamee's, just the two of us, was after the spring cleaning. That's another thing I hate about being at the grammar school – no more being kept off school to help Mammy with the cleaning. Mammy says I have to knuckle down and work hard, especially since I failed the 11-Plus and they have to pay fifty pounds for the first year's fees. She just expects me to get the scholarship at the end of the year. What if I don't? What if I couldn't care less if Henry the Sixth (or is it the Eighth?) had a million wives and I'm not able to learn all their names by heart?

Mammy's getting into the car and I'm standing like a statue on the footpath. She starts the engine and winds down the window.

'Well? Come on, in you get.'

I'm opening the door when Niamh comes running like the hammers of hell over to Mammy.

'Where are yous going? Can I come?'

Normally I'd be annoyed at her – she's always trying to butt in when Mammy and me are having a talk about something – but for some reason I wouldn't mind her coming with us today. Maybe the signs are coming back again.

'Yeah, Niamh can help with the groceries too and she can have half of my pastry,' I say. But Mammy's having none of it and is telling Niamh to keep an eye on the boys. She reverses the car, rolls the window back up and moves off, leaving Niamh with a big, cross face on her – not that that's too hard for our Niamh to manage. She was born with grouchy jowls.

We drive the whole way down town without saying a word, except when Mammy sees she's going to get stopped at the army post and suddenly realises she's left her licence in her other bag. But the soldier only asks where we're heading and lets us move on. We park up by Devenny's Grocery Store.

'Let's go and have that cup of tea first,' she says, and I'm thinking *Oh God* but I say 'Em ... okay.'

I love the smell of McNamee's Bakery, which you have to walk through to get to the café upstairs. We only buy things there on special occasions because it's daylight robbery. But their stuff is hard to beat, especially the potato bread and their apple turnovers with fresh cream inside. I should be feeling excited about my treat but I'm not.

The place is all done up now after the bomb in Jones's Shoe Store wrecked it. I think I liked the old café better. It's a bit empty so we have our pick of where to sit and Mammy goes to the back where there's a table for two in the corner. We take off our coats and she hangs them on one of the hooks over by the toilets. She sits down again but doesn't take off her hat because her hair is a mess. She lifts the menu and asks me what I fancy and I say an apple turnover. She says I can have a drink of something as well but tells me to stop picking the life out of the skin around my fingernails. So I say sorry and put my hands, spread out, on the table.

I can't help picking at them. I don't want to, it's just a habit. Sometimes, when I go too far and make them bleed, I stop for a bit because it's so sore, but then I'm back at it again. Mammy used to tell me I'd get gangrene, and even showed me photos from a library book. I had nightmares about it in the beginning. But it still didn't stop me. Now I know fine well I'm not going to get gangrene. Come to think of it though, I wasn't doing it as much when I thought I was getting the signs.

I tell Mammy I want a Coca-Cola and she asks would I not rather have a glass of milk or a cup of tea. So I say that I don't mind (which is not true) and she orders an apple turnover and a pot of tea for two. When I ask her why she's not having a pastry she says she's too full, which is not like Mammy, who is never too full when it comes to sweets. I go to the toilet because I think I have diarrhoea, but I don't, and when I come back the lady is bringing us our tea.

'That will be twenty pence, Mrs Reilly. You can pay on your way out if you like.'

But Mammy hands over the exact amount she has already taken from her purse.

Now, I have to say I'm still feeling really weird about the way Mammy is going on. She's not herself at all. I tell her she can have some of my apple turnover and she tells me to eat away, and if there is any left over, it won't go to waste. So I get stuck in while she pours the tea. She fills my cup first, lots of milk and two spoonfuls of sugar, before pouring her own. I'm a quarter of the way through my pastry when she says, in her serious voice, that she wants to talk to me about something important.

A piece of the pastry nearly gets stuck in my throat. I can feel a reddener coming on.

I hate my white skin and rosy cheeks. Even a piddling reddener makes me look like a tomato head, and the more I think about the fact that my cheeks are blazing, the redder they go, even when I'm not embarrassed about anything. And it takes forever before I can cool down again. I'd started putting talcum powder on my face in the morning before going to school until Mammy told me to catch myself on because I looked like someone on their death bed.

I'm taking a couple of gulps of tea to wash down the pastry and Mammy waits for me to put the cup on the saucer before she goes on. I can see she's not cross, but my heart's pumping anyway.

'Sinead, I know there's something bothering you and it's making you moody. It isn't like you to be indoors so much, nor is it like you not to want to talk, which makes me think that maybe you yourself don't really know what's the matter with you. Am I right?'

Well, I'm not sure how to answer so it's a good job I've lifted my apple turnover and am taking another bite. I'm trying to think of what to say. Should I explain about the Calling? I don't want to because I'm not sure any more about the signs. But I needn't have worried – Mammy isn't expecting an answer.

'Look, Sinead' – she takes a sip of tea – 'what you're feeling is very normal.'

'Is it?' I say, surprised.

I lick a lump of apple and fresh cream off the side of my mouth.

'Yes, girls your age can start having moods and they're not sure what's going on inside their heads. I know I did, but no one talked about things like that in those days.' She's fidgeting with the teaspoon.

I've put my pastry down. I'm confused and I'm waiting for her to continue. I hadn't realised so many girls my age might think they have the Calling.

'But it's something you shouldn't worry about at all. Sometimes you can have a wee bit of pain with it but that's healthy.'

'What do you mean by "pain"?' I ask.

'A bit like having a cramp,' Mammy says. 'But sometimes there's no pain at all.'

'Why does God want us to have pain sometimes?'

'I don't know. You'll have to ask Him that one yourself,' Mammy says, laughing a bit. She's more relaxed now, probably because she realises I know all about it. I don't think she was expecting that.

'But how will I know if it's for real or not?' I continue. 'I want to have it, but I'm beginning to think it's not going to happen. I had some signs after I came back from the retreat but then they went away and now I'm not sure any more.'

'What kind of signs? Sinead, you should have told me.' Now she's getting all concerned.

Well, I'm hardly going to be telling Mammy about the Freeman's catalogue and I feel my cheeks getting hotter still. Luckily for me, though, Mammy is clever and understands I'm a bit uncomfortable.

'There's no need to be embarrassed. It's normal until things sort themselves out. It's just your body changing,' she says.

This I don't get, but I ignore it because there's only one thing I'm interested in.

'Yes, but how will I know – for sure, sure – that I have it and it won't go away again?'

Mammy smiles and reaches over to push my glasses up on my nose.

'Oh, trust me, Sinead, you'll know when you have it and it's not going to go away. But you might not know for ages yet. One day you think it's coming and then it doesn't. That's just the way it is. So there's absolutely no point in worrying. You have to forget all about it now, and when it happens, it happens. There's no reason to be afraid about anything, okay?'

'Okay,' I say.

All of a sudden I feel great. I'm going to forget about the Calling altogether, like Mammy says. If it comes, it comes. And in the meantime, I'm going to try to be a better person to prove to God that I'm worthy. I think I was expecting it to happen too quickly. That was my mistake. I'm sure God wants to see how well I can cope with temptation. Didn't he send his own son into the desert for forty days and forty nights to test him? He's hardly going to come to a decision about me inside a couple of weeks, is he now?

I'm so relieved that I give Mammy a hug after we put our coats on. I used to hug her more when I was younger but recently I feel stupid clinging on to her like a baby. I still love the way she smells though.

We're in the car, halfway across the bridge, when I shout out that we've forgotten the groceries.

'It's all right,' she says. 'I'll send your father down with Niamh. You can go with them if you want.'

But I don't want to go with them. I'm going to call at Donoghue's to see if Claire wants to play kerb ball with me for a while before Doctor Who starts.

III. Mairead

Jesus Christ, Sinead, the door! Go easy on the bloody car door. How many times does she have to be told?

Sinead is already skipping down the estate.

Of course, Mairead is not annoyed with Sinead. They've spent a lovely hour together. It's the sudden noise that has aggravated her. That and the mood swing that came from passing Grainne Cunningham on her way back from town. Luckily, Grainne hadn't seen her, otherwise Mairead would have had to give her a lift. It's enough that they have to play bridge together. Mairead would never let herself down by showing she has even noticed the way Grainne has being going on these last months, pouting and flirting with any man who shows a bit of pity for her predicament.

Mairead has the steering wheel in a tight grip. Tension worms its way along her arms and across her chest. Releasing the steering wheel, she wrenches the key from the ignition and snatches her handbag from the back seat of the car. It's bulky on her lap, so bunged full that the clip doesn't close. She hurls the key in and rummages for a handkerchief somewhere amidst her purse, bills and sets of tangled rosary beads. But it's not there. It should be. She knows categorically that it should be.

Damn it.

The cuff of her coat relieves her itching nostrils.

Damn it.

She yanks out her oversized purse. There is definitely a bloody hanky in this bloody bag somewhere. But she can't find it. The urge to screech is mounting again. She can visualise her huge, gaping mouth, with its missing back tooth, devouring faces: Paddy's, her mother's, the grocer's, the milkman's, the man from the Provident's – and the children's, sometimes even the children's. She's a monster, that's what she is.

She stares out across the Green. Christ, get a grip. What must Eileen be going through? Those are real problems. The passenger door creaks open.

'Hey, are you all right?'

Paddy is standing with the baby in his arms. He's frowning.

'I was just thinking about poor Geraldine. It's desperate, the whole situation,' she replies.

Shauna is smiling and flapping her hands in anticipation of Mairead taking her. She is beautiful with her hazel eyes and fluffy, ginger hair – so like Paddy's side of the family to look at.

'We were beginning to think you'd dozed off, isn't that right, Shauna?' Paddy jokes over the roof of the car as she gets out.

A placid grin is the best Mairead can muster while she locks the car door.

'Has she eaten?' she asks, coming round to the footpath to take Shauna from Paddy.

'Yep, fed and changed. The rest of them have eaten too. They're all in there. I think I'll go over to Eileen's and see how the land lies,' Paddy starts to move off towards the Green.

'Will you be long?'

But either Paddy hasn't heard her or he's pretended not to. Paddy the Saint – he might deserve to be canonised if he didn't expend so much energy skirting his own responsibilities in his crusade to solve other people's problems. God, he can be so frustrating at times. People don't say 'Charity begins at home' for nothing, do they. She should call him back and tell him to go down town for the messages but Molly McElroy has just opened her door to put out her empties. The critter is getting frailer by the day.

'Ach, would you look at the size of her,' Molly lisps. Poor Molly rarely bothers to put in her dentures these days. Her gums are too sore.

Shauna is pretending to be shy and is burrowing her head in Mairead's neck.

'How are you keeping, Molly?' Mairead asks.

'Ah, can't complain, Mairead. Me back's been a bit sore but I'm on stronger tablets now. It just takes a wee while for them to start working.'

'Do you need anything from town? Paddy'll be going down shortly.'

'No, pet, you're all right. There's far too much in there. Annie May called in with a bag of stuff this morning. I don't know who she thinks'll be eating it all.'

Mairead is turning the key in the front door. She doesn't have time to stand and chat. 'Do you need a lift to Mass in the morning?'

'Naw, thanks pet, I'm not fit for it yet. Father Duncan's calling with me this evening, so he is. Cheerio, Shauna.' Molly moves further back into her front hall.

Mairead lifts Shauna's hand and flaps a wave. Drummore Drive won't be the same without Molly.

A sudden gust flings the door open before Mairead has a chance to let go of the key and she almost stumbles. Shauna's frightened limbs glue themselves to her body.

'It's okay, it's okay, we're fine,' Mairead says as she steadies herself and hobbles into the living room.

Damn it.

Niall has mounted the arm of the couch, ruler in hand, and is pretending to be John Cook riding Specify over the final fence in the Grand National. Niamh is making pained attempts to form stitches with the knitting needles and wool she got for her birthday. Eamon and Michael are watching *Tom and Jerry*. The air is chilly.

'Where's Kieran?' she asks Niamh.

'Dunno. Think he's gone upstairs.'

Mairead puts Shauna on the floor. The fire needs more coal. She goes to the scuttle. As expected, it's empty.

'Kieran, did your father not tell you to fill the scuttle?' she calls up the stairs.

No reply.

'Niamh, keep an eye on the baby,' she says and climbs the stairs. 'Kieran, did you not hear what I said?'

She pushes open the half-closed door. The room is empty. For a second, she gets distracted by the mess of unmade beds and pyjamas flung onto the floor. The upstairs cleaning is Sinead's and Niamh's job on a Saturday afternoon, but today she will probably end up doing it herself.

Where the hell is he?

She is hastily opening the window to air the room when she sees him standing at the back gate of the house talking to the Duffy boys. Banging on the window pane fails to attract his attention. For the love of God, Paddy, when are you going to do something about this? When he's shot dead like that young boy in Derry?

She batters down the stairs and marches through the living room, shouting at Niamh en route.

'Niamh, what did I tell you?'

Niamh jumps up. 'But I'm watching her,' she says and leaves her knitting to go sit beside Shauna on the floor.

Luckily, Shauna is contentedly playing with two dummies. She could have been over at the fire for all Niamh would have noticed. Why are the children so irresponsible?

Mairead opens the back door just as Kieran is unlatching the gate to go into the lane where the boys are moving off in the direction of town.

'Kieran, where are you going?' she calls out.

Kieran doesn't look at her, but the two boys turn their heads. She's reached the middle of the path and is repeating her question, though not quite as loudly as the first time. Kieran can't ignore her this time.

'Nowhere,' he says, glancing in her direction but avoiding eye contact. 'I'm just going to the bottom of the lane.'

'Well, come in and get your coat on first.'

'I'm not cold,' he says, closing the gate behind him.

The boys have moved further down the lane but are loitering.

'Well, I need you to go to Diver's for me anyway, so come on in until I make a list.'

'I'll go after,' Kieran says, looking at her with a definite don't-embarrass-me look.

But this is one time Mairead is not going to indulge teenage nonsense so she raises her voice, injecting a firm no-negotiation tone into it.

'No, Kieran, I need the messages now and you haven't filled the coal scuttle either. It's your job. The fire's nearly dead. Come on, hurry up.'

She's holding the gate wide open. There are seconds of silence. Would he have the nerve to defy her? But he raises his hand, signalling to the boys to go on without him and, head bent, rushes past her. He's nearly at the back door by the time Mairead has placed the latch on the gate.

Back in the house she finally removes her hat and coat.

'Mammy, Kieran swore at me and went upstairs just because I asked him what was wrong,' Niamh says, as Mairead places her hat on the sideboard and lays her coat over the back of a chair. Quite suddenly, exhaustion and its ancillary numbness kick in.

'Niamh, take your sister for a walk around the estate.'

She pulls Shauna's coat out from under the pram.

'Niall, out you go and take the boys with you. It'll be dark soon.'

Niall can't be bothered but he doesn't object. He rarely refuses her anything. There's a bond with him that she's never had with Kieran. Funny that, considering Kieran is her first. They say you're always closer to your first child. But no, out of the boys it's Niall who she gets on with better. Sometimes she takes him with her to the bingo. He's a star turn, keeping them all laughing between single lines and full houses.

'Kieran, can you come down here please?'

She has given up trying to fathom what goes on in

Kieran's brain. He's not your average teenager. Who reads philosophy at his age?

Going back into the scullery, she starts stacking the pile of dirty dishes. How many times has she told them to soak the plates after they've eaten? The sauce of the baked beans has well and truly hardened on plates, knives and forks. She'll need to scrape them, even after soaking. And the cups will need baking powder to remove the tea stains.

The living room door creaks and the TV goes on, her cue to go back into the living room. Kieran is sitting on the armchair, staring blankly at the loud screen. She's about to turn it off but adjusts the volume instead.

'You shouldn't have to be told to fill the scuttle. You're not asked to do much, so it shouldn't be so hard to remember the one thing that you're asked to do. It's called being responsible, Kieran. Lately I'm beginning to think you've forgotten what the word "responsibility" means.'

She's trying very, very hard to keep the sarcasm to a minimum. Kieran's reaction is proof that she's failed.

'I know fine well what responsibility means and it means a lot more than filling a coal scuttle.'

He stands and grabs the scuttle.

There's nothing to be gained by continuing this line of conversation. She sits on the sofa and tells him the coal can wait. He hesitates before putting the scuttle back down and slumping into the armchair.

'Look, Kieran, I've told you I don't want you hanging around with the Duffys. You know that.'

'First, I don't *hang around* with the Duffys. Sometimes we meet and just talk about things. For your information, they're not thugs. They know more about Irish history than I do—'

'No one says they're thugs, Kieran. It's just that they—'

'You call them thugs. I heard you the other day talking to Daddy,' Kieran interrupts.

Mairead is lost for something to say.

'I'm not a wain, you know. You embarrassed me outside in front of them. And just so you know, I can tell when someone is a thug and when they're not.'

'Look, I didn't mean to say that. It's not what I meant. It's just that their whole family is involved in politics and maybe the IRA and—'

'And so? What's so bad about that? At least they're trying to do something to end the tyranny that's existed in this country for hundreds of years.'

Mairead swallows hard against the lump forming in her throat and bites down hard on her lip. Saliva is slow on the uptake, forcing her tongue to lodge in the roof of her mouth. Kieran is giving a speech, like something out of a book, with a passion that terrifies her. This is not her son talking! The sense of danger is palpable and there's absolutely nothing she can do to redirect his energy and take control. Nothing, that is, without dogmatically putting her foot down and alienating him further. She lets him go on until panic gets the better of her and she finds her voice.

'That's enough, Kieran. Stop it! Stop it this minute!' she screeches, standing up and slamming the palm of her hand on the table instead of Kieran's face. 'There's going to be no more discussion about it. You're not allowed to have anything to do with that family. Do you hear me? Nothing. If I catch you anywhere near those boys, I swear to God, I'll not let you outside the door again. I mean it. You're too young to understand, but one day you'll thank me.'

Her cheeks are pulsating, as are the veins on the side of her forehead.

Kieran's mouth is still open but his words are welded by silence and frustration. He should let his tears spill. Kieran doesn't cry. He needs to cry. Everyone needs to cry. But his mouth has already closed shut and his jaw has tightened before she has a chance to soften. Without another word or a second glance, he lifts the coal scuttle. She's about to obstruct him, force a response, when Paddy and Sinead walk into the living room.

'In the name of God, what is going on Mairead? We could hear you from outside,' Paddy asks, his eyes flitting back and forth between her and Kieran, who doesn't look at anyone as he heads out to the coal shed.

The disapproval in Paddy's voice is loud and clear. Well, he'd better not think he can come in here playing God Almighty. If he'd done as they'd agreed, she wouldn't have had to get involved. She'd bet her right arm he's said sweet damn all to Riordan Duffy. Mairead's sick of worrying herself to sleep about this.

'There's nothing wrong, Paddy. Nothing whatsoever. Sinead, go find Niamh and tell her to come on in. You both need to get up those stairs and start the cleaning.'

Sinead is out the door in a flash and Paddy sits down at the table. He is unbuttoning his coat.

'I need you to go down to Devenny's and collect the groceries,' Mairead says.

'Are you going to tell me what on earth is going on, Mairead?'

His voice is devoid of its earlier tone, which is just as well because she's at the end of her tether with the whole lot of them.

'Enough of this nonsense about Kieran being allowed to come to his own conclusions, Paddy. He's too young to know what's what. That's the end of it. No more contact with those Duffy boys.'

Paddy goes to speak but she's having no more ifs and buts.

'He was about to go for a walk with them again. I've told him, from here on in if I find out he's been talking to any of them, he won't be allowed outside that door.'

Does she expect Paddy to agree with her? Of course not. They've been through it all umpteen times. And Paddy does what Paddy does best when he can't fight his corner: he says nothing. Because saying something might mean having to do something. Not Paddy's strong point when it comes to problems that are exclusively related to his own family.

Kieran has come back into the living room and is placing the scuttle on the hearth. Paddy can scowl as much as he likes. Scowling is dead easy.

She goes into the scullery and turns off the gas ring. The tea will have turned to tar by now. Leaning into the draining board, she stares out the window where a sudden downpour has transformed the pane of glass into a multitude of raindrop prisms. A foot patrol of young soldiers is passing along the back lane, their eyes darting right and left, rifles in readiness to counter any elusive sniper.

'Where's the car key?' Paddy calls out.

She goes back into the living room, lifts her bag and fumbles with the clip. Her hand is trembling as it digs out the key.

'Do you want to come for the run, Kieran?' Paddy asks, snapping the key from Mairead.

'He's alright where he is,' Mairead interjects, clicking

her bag shut. 'I need some help here with the baby. There's been nothing done today.'

She takes her time placing the handbag on the sideboard and adjusting some ornaments. Then she turns and heads back to the scullery, closing the door on them both, but not before she's glimpsed the anger on Kieran's face as he watches Paddy get ready to leave the house without him.

DECEMBER
1971

I. Mairead

In the dream, ten-year-old Mairead is always stooped over the flower beds when she hears the crunch of bicycle wheels on the gravelled path leading to the front of the house. She stands up and, turning round, sees the policeman dismount his bike. He parks it carefully against the pebble-dash. Theirs is a grand house with its latticed bay windows and tall chimneys looking down over the river.

Wisps of summer breeze, slipping through gaps in the hedge, are tickling her skinny calves and teasing the pleats of her favourite skirt. Officer Dudley hasn't noticed her standing at the far end of the garden. He is straightening his hat and smoothing down his jacket, tugging at the hem. Sometimes his back is turned, sometimes it isn't, but he always adjusts his cap one last time before reaching for the solid brass knocker.

Flimsy chrysanthemum petals and damp clay stick to her fingers. She is rubbing them on her gardening apron as she walks barefoot across the spiky grass. Her sandals are sitting neatly side by side near the path. They are new; she doesn't want to get them stained. She has just picked them up when the front door opens and she sees her mother with baby Sean in her arms. Her mother isn't smiling politely as she should be.

Mairead is standing very still, a sandal dangling from each hand. Her gaze is fixed on Officer Dudley, who is now speaking. She can't hear what he's saying. He's too far away. But his lips are still moving when the baby is dropped. Officer Dudley is fast, catching baby Sean seconds before his tiny, bald head would surely have smashed against the doorstep.

Nothing is moving. Micro-seconds of tranquillity.

Until her mother lets out a wail so fierce that Mairead's hands are forced open and the straps of her sandals slide from her fingertips onto the grass. Covering her ears, she stumbles back towards the hedge. She is trying to run in reverse, but her legs are leaden and her feet anchor her to the ground. The wail comes at her, envelops her, presses hard against her tightened lips. Her chest is aching, pain escalating by the second. She can no longer breathe. She must open her mouth. She shouldn't, but she must or she will surely die. And that is when the wail prises open her lips and swoops down into her stomach where it stays, bludgeoning her insides.

The trapped scream snaps the adult Mairead into consciousness. It always does, eventually. Minor details can change in the dream, like the sun not always shining or the lawn being overgrown, or her hair being in a plait instead of lying loose down her back. But with each replay of the day her father got killed there is no escaping the wail.

Mairead's body is damp, her scalp tingling, and she tightens her eyes shut against the onslaught of obsessive thoughts that follow her wakening. Like a river crashing through ineffectual banks, her intrusive thoughts forge on with an intensity undiminished by the passage of time.

There shouldn't be so much resentment after all these years. Her father had been an honest man, a hard-working man. Everyone said so. And isn't that what matters? There are no pictures, but she remembers him – tall, lean, quiet and mostly dressed in his Sunday best. They rarely saw him on the other days.

Her mother, at thirty-three, would have ended up on the shelf if it hadn't been for her father. The irony of it all. Oh yes, Thomas Boyle, a widower with three adult children, was a catch, even at fifty-two. Some catch.

Only imbeciles never make a will. It's easier to forgive a young imbecile, but a sixty-three-year-old one? So what if he had 'the constitution of an ox', if he would have 'lived until he was a hundred', as her mother repeated over and over in those early years? Accidents happen. Buses crush bicycles, dismember their careless riders. And this particular rider, this stranger who had lived with them, owned their house, their land, their other properties, had left them penniless. Her own father had done that to them. What, did he just *assume* Thomas Patrick Boyle Junior would do the honourable thing when he inherited the whole dammed lot? Did he even care? And what the hell did it matter if the town ostracised her half-brother? Yes, all very commendable on the part of the community, but it hadn't put money in their pockets. They still had the hardship, and worse – their mother's rigid, saintly acceptance of their fate.

Jesus Christ, she could have done something, her mother. It wasn't the Middle Ages they were living in. There were lawyers, for the love of God, courts. But no, oh no. Margaret Mary Boyle had to turn the other cheek and put her faith in the Lord Almighty, trudging the half mile to nine o'clock Mass every bloody morning like their lives depended on it.

Mairead opens her eyes to the blackness of the bedroom and shuts them immediately. The scream has retreated into her semi-consciousness where it belongs, but her emotion is now heading for a malignant turn. Her mouth is dry. *Hail Mary full of grace, the Lord is with thee* ... The prayer has worked in the past. *Blessed art thou amongst women and blessed is the fruit of thy womb, Jesus.* If she chants it over and over again ... *Hail Mary full of grace* ... God Himself will come to her rescue with a firm, but warranted disapproval of her unchristian thoughts.

When the sigh finally exits her body, her breathing settles into a peaceful rhythm. Yes, things could have been worse. They survived, didn't they? Baby Sean even managed to become a grammar school teacher.

Now wide awake, Mairead has become aware of the cold sneaking in around her exposed nightdress. Gently tugging at the blankets which Paddy has in his grip, she tucks them under her body and turns on her side, her buttocks grazing Paddy's. She closes her eyes. Getting back to sleep isn't going to be easy.

Death always triggers the dream, and with two wakes inside ten days to attend, it isn't surprising the dream has resurfaced. Molly McElroy passing away was expected; it was a wonder she'd held on for so long. But Grainne Cunningham's suicide has shaken her. The shock of it caused Mairead so much guilt that it brought on a migraine attack she'd been sure would debilitate her for days, as it usually did. Fortunately, it was short-lived. Only the dullest of aches has lingered. Nothing she can't tolerate.

Nobody would understand why she might feel so ashamed because no one knew how she had come to resent Grainne. No one but Grainne herself could have picked up on Mairead's subtle put-downs. She patronised the woman in the way only another woman can.

Of course, it wasn't difficult to make Grainne feel inferior. Mairead was by far the better bridge player. Even Paddy couldn't always hide his impatience when Grainne made her silly bids and counter bids. Not that that should ever be a reason for disliking someone.

Mairead reverts to lying on her back, opening her eyes to focus on a sliver of moonlight that has spliced the top of the curtains. Slowly, her vision adjusts and the outlines of familiar objects take their positions – the expensive dressing table she'd bought in a summer sale, the linen basket under the window, the solid wood wardrobe she'd been lucky to get for a third of the price. You could barely see the scratches on the cornice. It had been a bargain, no question about it. She trawls her gaze across the ceiling, momentarily getting her eyes tangled in the gaudy beads that adorn the rim of the lampshade, a wedding present she has to make do with.

The kick to her gut draws her eyelids shut again. She is dreading the wake. The funeral on Thursday doesn't bother her, but the wake … if only she could get out of it.

She turns on to her other side to face Paddy's curved back. The silken hem of the blanket is resting on the corner of his shoulder. Its movement is barely discernible so peaceful is his sleep. She can make out the tiny patch of shiny scalp in the half darkness and for some reason she finds herself wanting to touch it. It's his vulnerable spot. Going bald terrifies him. She moves closer and is soothed by the warmth radiating from his entire body. He too has been in a daze since the news of the suicide. Paddy had felt very sorry for Grainne when her husband did the midnight flit, though sometimes his concern for 'Poor Grainne' bordered on stupidity. Okay, so the woman's husband ran off on her. It's not the first nor the last time it's happened to someone. People get over it … and without losing their self-respect in the process.

Why is she being so harsh? Oh, that she could be more like Paddy. He's a better person than she is. When Grainne wanted to quit the bridge club it was Paddy who persuaded her to continue, even giving her lessons to improve her game. Paddy is drawn to unfortunate souls, the underdogs of this world. He can't help it. And Grainne fit that description to perfection. It wasn't that Mairead felt no compassion for the woman, but the fact is, Paddy can be naive and sometimes she had been concerned that his kindness might have been misconstrued by the town, what with the reputation Grainne had acquired, as well as the fact that Grainne had started to take Paddy's kindness a wee bit for granted.

Paddy is right, though. People shouldn't be guided by idle gossip. He has a way of making Mairead feel guilty when she voices her opinion too strongly. Not that she had made much out of the Grainne thing in front of him, or anyone for that matter. Nothing riles Paddy more than insinuation, especially when he's being a hell of a lot more Christian than most people in the town, including herself.

She heaves herself on to her back again, wishing Paddy would wake up. She wants to talk about how badly she feels, get it off her chest before facing Grainne in her coffin. What must it be like for the family, no proper funeral? Paddy might be right about that one. The Catholic Church shouldn't be so hard on the family left with the bereavement. But then again, he can't have it both ways, which was more or less the point Mairead had been trying to make yesterday morning: 'It's based on the same principle, Paddy. Only God can give or take life. When people take things into their own hands, it's sacrilege as far as the Church is concerned.' That's all she had said. As usual, though, she had lost her train of thought. Paddy is so much more articulate than she is and when he starts to get impatient, because she goes off at tangents explaining what she means, her tongue gets tied and it all comes out wrong. That morning, he'd just ended up getting annoyed and refused to continue the conversation. In his opinion, Mairead was being manipulative, and it was in bad taste to refer to that particular bone of contention.

But when is it ever the right time? No matter how much she pressurises him to use contraception he refuses. It's against his ethics, his 'moral code', which she could respect more if she didn't have to live in constant fear of pregnancy. Knowing her luck she'll end up like Annie Coyle, who's expecting her thirteenth child and her nearly forty-five years of age.

Mairead twists back round on to her other side and puts her arm around Paddy, moulding her groin into his buttocks. She's aware that if he wakes up, and he probably will, she'll have to do it. But it'll be worth it – she can talk to him afterwards. She's due in a few days, so she's almost certain it's safe.

Paddy is very sensitive to rejection so she tries, as much as she can, to avoid making him feel that way. Unfortunately, he can't cuddle without getting all worked up. It's a pity.

She would love to be able to cuddle more. But the way it is, she holds back a lot of the time for fear of him getting the wrong idea. They've talked about it a wee bit and he seems to understand at the time, but then he forgets, so she just goes without. Less hassle. After all, she can hardly announce: 'I want a cuddle but none of the other please.' She has tried a few times in a jokey way, but it doesn't work. Men just need it more and that's the height of it. No point in fighting about it all the time. But she does wish men were more like women in this department.

She nuzzles the nape of Paddy's neck and he stirs, pressing against her. She presses too, and he turns slowly on to his back. He likes to be wakened from sleep this way, unlike her. How anyone likes to be wakened from a deep sleep is beyond her.

It isn't that she doesn't get aroused easily enough, but she needs time to get into it. Sometimes, he makes the effort to please her but it can take her ages. If it takes too long it can put him off a bit, and when that happens it's so awkward. Like the kissing and the cuddling, it's just easier sometimes not to expect too much.

Paddy's breathing is getting heavier. He turns his head and pecks her forehead. Mairead frees her hand and brings it up to turn Paddy on his side so they can find each other's mouths. She's on her back before she knows it, trying to position herself so the bedsprings don't creak too much.

The bed needs dumping. It would have lasted a lifetime if Paddy didn't insist on letting the children jump on it every two seconds. And that lampshade definitely has to go. Even one of those plain ones in Woolworths would be better and it wouldn't break the bank, though the colour is a bit of a problem. They only come in white and beige. Strong colours, like maroon or jade green, are much better. She's seen one in Delaney's – a beautiful, rich purple – but it costs an arm and a leg. Well, they do say you get what you pay for. If you can afford quality, you can afford choice.

When Paddy rolls on to his back again she reaches under the mattress for the squashed toilet roll. After she sorts herself out, she cuddles up to him. He's still on his back, kneading his forehead. The first glimmer of dawn is pushing through the gaps in the curtains. Paddy's eyes are open, staring at the ceiling. He doesn't draw her close, so she puts her arm around his midriff and rests her cheek against his arm.

'Are you thinking what I'm thinking?' she asks.

When she gets no response, she goes on.

'Grainne Cunningham's wake ... I wish we didn't have to go, Paddy. I don't know if I can face it.' She wants to tell him how guilty she feels but how is she going to explain it? 'Could you not just go for the both of us?' she asks.

There's a pause.

'If only one of us is to go, it should be you, Mairead. You were her bridge partner,' Paddy says, almost in a whisper. He stops kneading his brow and pulls the blankets up under his chin.

'I suppose, but you did play with her those times in the mixed pairs when I couldn't come for one reason or another.'

He's not buying it.

'Look, either we both go or neither of us goes,' Paddy says, turning his back to her. Mairead's arm is now lying limply on his waist, her palm resting on the curve of his belly. She wants to talk more but he's pulled himself nearer to the edge of the bed, positioning his pillow accordingly. Her palm retreats to his waist before she turns on her back.

She adjusts her nightdress, pulling it down over her knees. She takes her share of the blankets and tugs them up over her shoulder as she turns on to her other side. Her head finds a comfortable indent near the edge of the pillow and she glances at the shadowy Sacred Heart picture on the wall before closing her eyes.

It won't be easy getting back to sleep.

II. Sinead

'Sinead, I think it's starting to snow,' Kieran calls out from the scullery on his way to the bathroom.

I'm sitting at the table in the living room and I'm stupid enough to believe him; Christmas isn't the same without snow. As I open the venetian blinds to take a look I don't see any sign of snow, but I get an eyeful of Marty Donnelly charging across the Green to our house. He's got his anorak hood up and his head down as if he's a bull chasing a matador. Marty is hilarious, even when he isn't trying to be funny. He has these long, spindly legs that look ridiculous, but Daddy says he's got the speed of a professional sprinter. Daddy's right because it's only a matter of seconds before Marty comes barging in, out of breath.

'Hey, where's Kieran?' he shouts. He's pulled down his hood and is trying to undo the zip in his anorak.

'Keep your voice down, Marty. The wee ones are asleep,' I say in a stern voice. I've been left in charge because

Mammy and Daddy had to go to a wake in Derry. 'Kieran's in the loo.'

'Shush,' says Niall.

Niall and Niamh are sitting on the couch watching *Meet Me in St. Louis* for the third time. It was on last year, and the year before. I'm sick of it.

'Yeah, shush,' Niamh pipes up, looking at me with her growly face. 'We can't hear what they're saying.'

'Don't tell me to shush,' I shout back. Niamh's getting too big for her boots as far as I'm concerned. 'Anyway, you're not allowed to stay up and that film isn't over for ages.'

'Who says we can't stay up? We've no school tomorrow,' says Niall.

'I say, that's who. So be quiet, the both of you.'

'Sinead, stop bossing everyone about,' Kieran calls from the scullery on his way into the living room. 'I'm the eldest. I'll say when they have to go to bed. Yous can stay up,' he says, turning to Niamh and Niall.

Kieran is pretending not to notice that I'm about to burst a blood vessel. The flamin' nerve of him, acting the hard man with me. He does damn all around the house so he's got no business trying to show he's the king of the castle when Mammy and Daddy aren't around. But I say nothing because if we start quarrelling, Mammy will get upset that we started a rumpus when we promised we'd behave ourselves. And our Niall would be chomping at the bit to tell her.

'How's it going, Marty?' Kieran says.

'Hey there, Kieran, how's yourself?' replies Marty, finally managing to get his anorak off.

'Not so bad, if I didn't have to listen to Ollie over there.'

'Ha, ha, Kieran. Get yourself a new joke. Oh yeah, but that might mean you need to know the definition of humour,' I say and turn away from him.

Kieran thinks it's so, so funny. I look nothing like Ollie from *On the Buses*. Except for the thick glasses.

Marty nods in the direction of the television. 'They're watching that stupid film over in our house too,' he says. 'Hey, Niall, do you not want to watch the other channel?'

'Aye, Niall, what're you watching that sissy movie for anyway? Haven't you already seen it a million times?' Kieran says, going towards the television. He's got that sly look on his face that gets everyone's back up.

Now I'm pleased Niamh is getting too big for her boots because she leaps off the settee at the speed of lightning and stands between the TV and Kieran, her arms stretched out over the screen and the control panel.

'Don't you dare change the channel, Kieran,' she screams.

It wouldn't be so bad if Kieran actually wanted to watch the television himself. But it's all just an act. He wants to impress Marty and show he's the boss. Even Marty knows that Kieran is just being a bully.

'Ach, it doesn't matter, Kieran. Sure, there's probably nothing on worth watching anyway,' Marty says.

But Kieran doesn't budge. He tries to frighten Niamh by putting his face so close to hers that their glasses nearly touch. I get up from the table and am about to tackle him when there's an almighty banging on our front door.

For a few seconds no one moves. Then there's even louder banging, which starts me shaking. I don't know why but I get behind Kieran, who's turned towards the window. Marty would have been a safer bet. It's him who's brave enough to actually go over to the window and open the blinds. The three of us peer out and see an army tank parked on our kerb; two soldiers with rifles are crouched down at the side of it. There's another soldier standing halfway down our front path with a walkie-talkie in his hand. Suddenly he drops to the ground and all three soldiers point their rifles at the window.

I screech and duck.

'Shut the blinds, Marty!' Kieran shouts.

By now, Niamh has started to blubber and Niall is hiding behind an armchair. I'm trying to get Niamh to calm down and Kieran is telling me to put a sock in it. I bloody hate it when he says that. Niall is whispering stupid questions from over the top of the armchair when Marty tells us all to shut up, which we do – for about ten seconds. Then we hear the back door opening.

'Kieran, do something!' I don't mean to squeal. It just comes out.

Of course, it's enough to set Niamh off again. But I've no time to say anything else because the next thing I know there's a soldier in our scullery calling out, 'This is the British army and we're coming in.' Well, that's enough to shut us all up and we're standing, fixed to the spot, when the soldier appears at the scullery door, rifle pointed. It doesn't take him long to figure out there are no adults around.

'Where are your parents?' he asks, taking two small steps into the living room.

His eyes are darting all over the place, just like soldiers do in the movies. Then he looks at Marty, obviously because he's the oldest in the room. A second soldier has followed him but is standing inside the scullery.

'I'm a cousin. I don't live here,' Marty replies in a shaky voice. 'Kieran, where have they gone?'

'It's none of their business where they've gone,' Kieran answers.

I can't believe Kieran has actually said that – and neither can Marty from the look on his face. What the hell is the matter with Kieran? Does he want to get us all killed?

'They are at a wake in Derry,' I pipe up without thinking, and Kieran looks at me like I've divulged some great family secret.

'Can you keep your mouth shut for once, Sinead?' He's not asking me; he's ordering me. God, I think I'm more scared of Kieran than I am of the British soldiers.

Soldier Number One is gradually making his way across the living room to the front door, all the while eyeballing Kieran.

'What's your name, lad, and how old are you?' he asks. His voice is very calm and his accent is like my cousins', who live in Manchester.

Of course, wouldn't you know, Kieran refuses to answer. Now he's just being ridiculous. He's lucky the soldier totally ignores him and turns to Marty instead.

'What's your name? Was it you who ran across the Green?'

I can see that Marty's getting really scared now.

'Don't answer him,' Kieran shouts and moves towards Marty.

'Stand back! Both of you, over by the television,' Number One orders. His voice isn't as nice as it was before.

Marty immediately does as he's told and Kieran follows him, though he doesn't rush himself. Then the soldier opens our front door and lets in Soldier Number Three, the one who we'd seen outside on the footpath.

I glance at Kieran, who's grinding his teeth the same way

he used to just before he had a petit mal. He hasn't had one for ages. If he has one now, I swear I'll faint.

What happens next, though, nearly makes me faint anyway. Kieran takes off his glasses and stares right into the soldier's eyes. Well, I'm assuming that's what he's trying to do because without his glasses he can't see his finger in front of him, never mind a pair of eyes. But he's looking in the right direction anyway – the soldier doesn't know he's as blind as a bat.

'You have no legal right to be in this house or this country,' Kieran says like a spokesman for Sinn Féin. What in the name of God has possessed him? I mean, who talks like that at his age?

We're staring at him and Marty's about to speak, I think, when Soldier Number Three asks who is upstairs. It's only then I hear the creak of the floorboards and realise the boys must be out of bed. That's when Shauna starts to cry.

'It's the wee ones. Can I go up and get the baby?' I ask, trying to steady my voice because I'm close to blubbering myself. I've been holding it in, unlike Niamh who has been sniffling and wiping snot with her sleeve the whole time.

'Let's go,' says Soldier Number One.

He looks a bit like Robert Mitchum.

I go into the hall and have to hold on to the banister going up the stairs because my legs are wobbly. The cold air is blowing in from outside where the front door is partly open. Robert Mitchum is following me and as soon as I reach the landing, I hear Michael and Eamon whispering behind their bedroom door.

'Come on out, boys, it's okay,' I say.

They don't appear so I have to go in and take them by the hand.

'It's all right, come on,' I say, and I tell them to wait while I go and lift Shauna who, I discover, is trying to climb out of her cot. I pick her up, grab her dummy, stuff it into her mouth and go back to the landing where I stand waiting for instructions, the boys hanging on to my dress.

Soldier Number Three is still at the foot of the stairs and Robert Mitchum is searching Mammy's room. When he comes out, he goes into the boys' room. I stay put and tell the boys to shush. Shauna is a bit dopey from having just woken up and she has her head on my shoulder. I hear the wardrobe doors opening and the clatter of hangers, then the drawers. I want to turn round but I just keep my eyes on the floor. The boys are dead quiet now. Finally, the soldier goes into my room.

When he's finished he calls down, 'Nothing up here.' Then he says to me in the kindest voice, 'Okay, we can start moving on down now. Watch your step there, luv.'

We pass Soldier Number Three at the front door to go into the living room. I tell the boys to join Niamh on the couch and to behave themselves. Niall is sitting on the armchair. I don't want to sit down but I have to because Shauna is far too heavy. Marty and Kieran are still standing by the table. Thank God Kieran seems to have calmed down a bit. Mammy is definitely right about his attitude. Recently, I think Mammy is right about a lot of things.

Anyway, Robert Mitchum has gone into the scullery and is banging about in drawers and cupboards when I hear Kieran say, under his breath, 'Limey bastards.' Jesus, Mary and Joseph. Just when my heart has come back up out of my stomach, Kieran has me sweating again. And to top it off, Shauna starts to whinge, then pulls her dummy out. She's getting her temper worked up and is calling for Mammy.

I whisper through gritted teeth, 'Kieran, if you don't cut it out, I swear to God I'll—'

But I'm interrupted by Soldier Number Two, who has moved from the scullery door to the sideboard, which he's trying to open.

'What's inside?' he asks. It's the first time he's spoken since the beginning of the raid.

'Nothing!' Kieran and I shout out at the same time. We look at each other in panic. Marty is staring at the pair of us.

'Where's the key?' asks the soldier.

'There is no key,' Kieran replies. 'It's lost.'

'Sarge, you might want to get back in here,' the soldier calls out to Robert Mitchum, who is still in the scullery.

I'm going to have a heart attack. Kieran doesn't have to say a word because I know what his eyes are telling me. It's okay. Just stick to the story. There is no key. It's lost.

Robert Mitchum has come into the living room.

'It's locked. They say the key is lost,' says the creepy soldier, pointing his rifle at the sideboard.

'Listen, tough guy,' the sergeant says, taking two quick strides to where Kieran is standing.

Marty side-steps away from Kieran, who hasn't moved as much as an inch.

'I've had enough of your lip,' the sergeant goes on. 'You can tell us where the key to that cupboard is or you can let us smash it open. It makes no difference to us. Either way we're going to open it.'

He's speaking slowly, a bit like the way Christopher Lee speaks just before he sinks his teeth in – if you can imagine Christopher Lee with a Manchester accent.

I'm terrified he's going to turn to me. But he doesn't.

And I'm so relieved when I hear Kieran speak in his best-behaviour voice.

'Honestly, we don't have the key. I didn't lie about that. But it's not lost. My mother has it with her all the time in her purse. I swear. I'm telling you the truth.'

The sergeant hasn't moved. He's still eyeballing Kieran.

'Then tell me, what does your mother keep inside her cupboard that she carries the key with her everywhere?'

'I don't know,' Kieran replies in a *very* convincing voice.

There's this really long silence while the soldier stares at Kieran, who manages to hold the stare. No one can beat Kieran at the staring game. He can go for ages without even blinking.

'I don't believe you. Corporal Higgins, smash it open,' the sergeant orders without taking his eyes off Kieran.

'No, don't,' shouts Kieran and he goes to push past. I can't believe how brave Kieran is. If it was me I'd have already blabbed.

But the sergeant isn't letting him go anywhere and he forces him back against the table.

'Okay, okay, I'll tell you, I'll tell you … but only if we can go into the scullery,' Kieran says.

There's a long pause. Then the sergeant raises his hand and for a minute I think he's going to slap Kieran. But I soon realise he's giving the go-ahead to Corporal Higgins.

The first smash of the rifle butt against the metal lock doesn't open the sideboard but it starts Shauna screaming. I squeeze her closer to me and look over to the couch where Niamh is sitting with the two boys on either side of her. Eamon and Michael have their hands over their ears and Niamh has her arms around them. The tears are tripping her. Niall is sitting like a zombie, staring into the fireplace.

I'm praying like mad. Please, please don't let the boys turn round.

I know that the second smash will open the sideboard doors. I don't want to look but I can't help myself. I'm not scared any more but I just wish Grainne Cunningham hadn't decided to die. I wish Mammy and Daddy would walk in the door. I wish Aunty Eileen would walk in the door. Anyone would do.

The first Santa Claus present to fall out of the sideboard is Michael's Celtic football. It bounces onto the floor and makes its way in smaller bounces towards the scullery. Eamon sees the ball before his own present hits the ground. His face is screwed up in confusion. He looks at me, then at Kieran. Kieran is staring straight ahead at nothing. Next comes Niamh's Sindy doll and Beano Annual, followed by Niall's magician's set. It doesn't matter so much about Niamh and Niall – they know there's no Santa. Shauna's teddy bear tumbles out last of all.

My bottom lip is sore from biting down on it but I don't cry.

No one moves until after all the soldiers are gone and the tank drives away.

III. Paddy

Paddy slows down and takes the bend in second gear. It's the last blind spot; only three more miles to go. With his chin jutting over the top of the steering wheel, his eyes squint and blink to the rhythm of the wipers so that the road is kept in focus. But a salty itch, now swelling under a membrane of drying fluid, draws his finger to the corner of his left eye where he pokes and rubs until relief comes.

Night fog and sleet: a driver's nightmare at the best of times, never mind when you're crippled with astigmatism.

In one way, though, the weather conditions are a godsend. They lend legitimacy to the silence in the car. And the sealed envelope grazing the lining of his coat pocket is pretending, at least for the moment, to have no significance.

He should have followed Mairead out of the wake house when he had the chance. Pausing on the doorstep, stepping back to let more people in – it was just bad luck. Otherwise he would have been in the car, on his way. If Grainne's sister had wanted him to have the envelope, she would have had to find another time and place to give it to him, plain and simple. She wasn't exactly being tactful, considering the circumstances of Grainne's demise. It wasn't that she didn't know where to find him if she needed to, for Christ's sake.

'Mr Reilly, thank you for coming, I didn't get a chance to speak to you earlier.'

Aileen had been standing close by before coming over to face him in the doorway. She glanced past him and raised her hand in a half wave to Mairead, who was waiting by the car parked on the other side of the road. Paddy had only met Aileen a couple of times before and he felt awkward. She was a younger, fresher-looking version of Grainne. There might not have been a wake at all but for Aileen. The sisters had been close; Derry families stick together.

His left eyelid had begun to tremor, a twitch that he might get stuck with for weeks.

'We weren't expecting such a big turnout, otherwise I would have come over earlier for a proper chat,' she went on, reaching into her jacket pocket and pulling out the envelope with 'For Paddy Reilly' scrawled across the centre. His hands had remained inert, like they were disowning him, refusing to abandon the warmth and safety of his coat pockets.

'Grainne left this for you, Mr Reilly. She didn't have many friends, as you probably know. She was grateful for your kindness, the bridge lessons and all.'

The sound of footsteps behind him triggered his left hand into action; he grabbed the envelope, shoving it into his pocket.

'Poor Grainne, we still can't believe it,' Paddy said.

Aileen was struggling to contain her grief. But to his

relief, another car pulled up outside the house, drawing her attention away from him and giving him enough time to make to leave.

'We'd best get back to the gang. They're on their own. We'll most likely see you at the burial tomorrow.'

'What was all that about?' Mairead asked as soon as the car turned the street corner towards the main road. 'What did she hand you? Aren't you going to open it?'

So much for hoping Mairead hadn't seen the envelope. But luckily for Paddy the sleet started falling thicker.

'God knows what was going on in Grainne's head before she swallowed those tablets. Wasn't she forever apologising and thanking people? Flipping wipers … they're useless. Grab that chamois, Mairead. You'll have to keep wiping the windscreen till the car heats up.'

With a bit of luck any further reference to the letter would be put on hold until they got home.

As they approach the outskirts of town, Paddy's body relaxes at the sight of the street lamps. Then he sees the road block. Oh, for the love of God, not again! They had been pulled in earlier, made to go through a rigmarole of ridiculous questioning.

Where are you headed, sir?

Where are you coming from, sir?

What is the address of the wake house, sir?

What time did you leave the wake house, sir?

What was the name of the deceased, sir?

They're getting carried away with themselves, these soldiers. You just can't be searching cars and stopping people in the streets willy-nilly. It's nothing short of harassment. And that moron Brian Faulkner has done the country no favours by bringing back internment. Only a fool could believe that putting a man in jail indefinitely and without a trial would squash the Provisional IRA and resolve the conflict in Northern Ireland. Has history taught them nothing? The entire Stormont government must have a brain the size of a pea if they can't see how that brilliant decision is going to blow up in their faces – literally as well as figuratively, unfortunately.

Paddy slows to a snail's pace and takes his place behind three cars waiting to be checked. He rolls down the window when his turn comes.

'There you go,' he says, handing over his licence. 'Is there something going on? This is the second block in ten miles.'

'Extra security on account of the prime minister's visit … Thank you, sir.'

Paddy takes back his licence. He'd clean forgotten Ted Heath was gracing this part of the United Kingdom in the name of peace and reconciliation. Oh, for Pete's sake, the man is a two-hour drive away in Belfast, that's if he isn't already on a plane home. Extra security – a load of hooey!

'That soldier's only a youngster,' Mairead says, propelling Paddy back to reality and forcing him into small talk. Any talk that can delay the inevitable is okay, though.

The car is veering off the main street to cross the bridge towards the Ballybeehan Road and another, more oppressive, silence has consumed the confined space of the car. Then the sudden appearance of an army Saracen on the narrowing road makes the car jolt and swerve into Billy Conway's driveway.

'Someone should tell those boys to slow it down a bit,' Paddy says, shifting gears and moving off towards Drummore Court. Feckin' eejits. Feckin' roads, feckin' weather, feckin' wakes …

'Do you want to read the letter before we go inside?' Mairead is asking as Paddy parks close to the kerb.

Feckin' women. Of course he doesn't want to read the feckin' letter before they go into the house. Right, he has to get his head in order if he's to find a way out of this mess. But then the front door of the house is flung open and Sinead comes running down the path. She is shouting and crying.

'Daddy, Daddy, the army has raided our house, so it has, and the sideboard's ruined and all the Santa toys were thrown on the floor.'

Paddy gets out of the car. Mairead has already reached the path and is rushing towards the entrance where Eileen is standing with Shauna in her arms.

It's not too often a man finds comfort in sheer confusion, but Paddy has just been handed a reprieve of sorts. He slams the car door and follows Mairead into the house, with Sinead sprinting on ahead of him. But whatever solace he gets is only temporary as the scene before him sends shock waves throughout his body. It's not the toys strewn over the floor that disturb him. It's his children's faces – Niamh's and the wee ones', tear-stained and terrified; Niall's and Sinead's, shaken and scared; Kieran's, aloof but angry. He can always read his son, glimpse behind the mask. Such a pity Mairead can't.

'We hadn't a clue, Paddy,' Eileen is saying, 'not until a couple of minutes ago. They saw Marty running across the green and got suspicious.'

Paddy hears the apology in his sister's voice. It isn't her fault, even if she had been asked to keep an eye out till they got back. He doesn't wait for her to finish her account.

'Paddy, come back. There's nothing you can do, for God's sake. It'll only make things worse,' Mairead is shouting.

But Paddy is already halfway down the path.

'Wait, wait, I'm coming with you,' she's calling after him, and this turns his eyes towards her, his hand gripping the car door.

'No, Mairead. Stay here with the children. I don't know how long this will take. They need you here.'

For once Mairead has the sense to acknowledge that he's right.

When Paddy pulls up outside the RUC barracks, he turns off the engine and reaches into his coat pocket. The letter is creased and one side of the seal has come unstuck. Running his forefinger under the flap of the envelope, he eases the other half open and feels inside to gauge the bulk of its contents. There are at least two pages but no more than three. He still hasn't removed the letter when the sound of an RUC jeep coming in the opposite direction distracts him. It's indicating a right turn into the barracks.

He folds the envelope in two and stuffs it into the glove compartment. The letter will have to wait. Taking the key from the ignition, he waits for the truck to go through the gates, held open by one of the officers, before getting out and locking the car door. The barracks is beginning to look more like a prisoner-of-war camp than a local police station. It'll take a hell of a lot more than a few ugly barbed-wire fences to stop the IRA.

He presses the bell on a newly constructed entrance gate for the public.

'Oh, how's it going, Paddy? What's up?' asks William McPherson, approaching the gate and inserting the big iron key into the lock.

The best cricket player this side of Tyrone was McPherson, back in the day. Paddy might have been a decent cricketer but William could hit the ball for six nearly every time. 'Willy the Wizard' they all called him.

'My house was raided tonight by the British army, with neither myself nor my wife at home. I mean, what is the country coming to when the army can just walk into any man's house and wreak havoc? Can you tell me that, William?'

It's just unfortunate that William McPherson happens to be on duty. But Paddy's rage is mounting, now that things are sinking in. No one is more of a pacifist than he is, but when lines are crossed, when lines are crossed …

'Whoa, slow down now, Paddy. Let's get inside out of this bloody cold and we'll try to get to the bottom of this,' William says, leading Paddy to the main building and into a small office off the public waiting area. 'Sit yourself down there and I'll be with you in a second,' says William, leaving him alone.

Paddy half follows him and stands at the open door, watching him disappear down the long corridor that joins the old building to the new. He spots Malachy McBride asleep on a chair, head against the wall, drunk as a coot again. Better there than lying in some ditch, freezing to death.

Back in the office the clock on the wall says nine fifty. He checks his watch; it can't be that late, can it? The room is bare but for three chairs and a desk. There's a draught coming through the old sash window that bites into the air and he draws his coat collar up round his neck. William's taking his time. Maybe Paddy should go find him, hurry him up a bit. Paddy's in no form for exercising restraint, even towards a civil being like William McPherson. Not under these circumstances. Not after the day he's had. No way.

But William appears in the nick of time with a sheaf of forms and a pen in his hand.

'Sorry there, Paddy, but I've had to spend the last hour getting yer man Malachy settled down and when the bell went I was heading for the loo at the other end of the corridor. Now remind me, where is it you live? And at what time exactly did the incident occur?'

'Drummore Court. Number Seven. But what odds is it about the time? Half an hour ago, maybe, I don't know. That's the point, William – I wasn't there! They raided a house full of youngsters, a house full of defenceless, terrified children, and I want the people responsible to answer to that.'

Paddy's fingers have curled into fists and his back teeth are grinding into his jaw bone. If William McPherson knows what's good for him, he'll come up with something more than a form to fill in, because it looks a bit like that's where Willy the Wizard is going with this one and Paddy is having none of it.

'So just tell me where to go to get some answers.'

'Look, hang on and I'll go make a call. Can I get you a cup of tea, Paddy?'

The last thing Paddy wants now is a cup of bloody tea. A drop of vodka, on the other hand …

'No, but thanks,' answers Paddy, deflated. He sits back down in his seat after William leaves.

Vodka. It's a hard drink to beat. But it's a curse – which is why he'll be drinking no more of the stuff come the New Year. He'll be sticking to the odd pint from there on in, if even that. For certain there'll be no more spirits. They mess with his head.

Definitely, without the shadow of a doubt, it was the vodka that got him into trouble with Grainne the first time.

After that, he had just felt sorry for her, didn't want to hurt her feelings. And vodka had turned Grainne into a semi-alcoholic, that's for sure. Otherwise, she wouldn't always have had a bottle stashed in the house. Poor Grainne! There was no saving her from herself. He had done his best. Harsh as it might sound, she's probably better off where she is.

Paddy's toes are feeling the nip. He hasn't the energy to hunt down William McPherson, but if he doesn't get the blood circulating in his feet they'll be in a state of rigor mortis soon. Standing very upright, like in the days when his mother thought he had the makings of an All-Ireland Dancing Champion, he raises himself up and down on his tiptoes until the numbness relents. These feet were made for football, not Irish dancing, but he couldn't have told his mother that at the time. Stubborn as a mule, she was. Not that he didn't like a jig, mind you, but he was useless at it. End of story. 'You're turning him into a bloody sissy. Is that what you want? You want him to be a laughing stock?' It wasn't often that Paddy's father raised his voice, and less often that anyone paid attention to it when he did. But after that, Paddy wasn't forced to go to Irish dancing classes any more.

He can hear footsteps coming along the corridor so he sits back down on the chair, rubbing his palms with vigour before driving both hands deep into their respective pockets, limbs tightly pulled in to conserve as much body heat as possible. William enters and drags a chair round to the other side of the desk.

'Right, Paddy, I called army headquarters and there's no official report yet, but it seems there was some suspicious activity and the army acted accordingly. As it turns out it was a false alarm but they had to follow the lead. Of course, the officer in command apologises for—'

'What are you on about? My nephew ran across the Green to our house. That's it. Was that the sum total of "suspicious activity"? I'd like to speak to these army hotshots, hear what they have to say.'

'They were only doing their job. They don't always get it right, but—'

'Look, I appreciate your diplomacy, but this is unacceptable. I want to lodge an official complaint. I'm going to prosecute.' It might be going against the grain for Paddy to be so unwilling to compromise, but when lines are crossed there's no way back. 'So give me whatever forms I have to fill in and let me get on with it. No offence intended, William – I know you're just doing your job.'

William takes his hat off and places it on the corner of the desk. He'll never need a hair piece that's for sure. And there's not a grey hair in sight. He's lifted the pen and is tapping it nervously on the pile of forms in front of him.

'You can fill out as many forms as you like, and I'm right behind you on that one, Paddy, but I'm telling you, you're wasting your time. They were acting within their legal rights. I'm sure you know as well as I do the power granted in the Internment Law. Now, I'm not saying there hasn't been a terrible mistake made. But legally they've done nothing wrong and that's the bottom line.'

William pushes a set of forms across the desk. 'You can fill them out here if you like, or take them home with you and come back tomorrow. It's up to you.' He places the pen alongside the papers.

Paddy looks at the official documents and the pen. He squeezes the sting from his eyes and then pushes himself out of the chair. Taking the forms, he folds them in two, pressing them into a deep crease.

'It's been a long day, William. I'll be down first thing tomorrow morning.'

'Right you are, Paddy. I'll not be here myself. We're doing Christmas in Ballymena this year. I'll be back on duty on the second of January.'

'Oh right. Well then, maybe I'll leave things till after the holidays – wait till you're back.'

'You've time enough anyway,' William says, moving towards the corridor where Malachy McBride is coming round and getting a bit obnoxious with it.

'You've your hands full with that fella, William.'

'Ach, tell me about it. The guard will let you out, Paddy.'

And with that William leaves him standing on his own.

'Have a good Christmas and New Year, William,' Paddy calls after him, heading for the exit.

'Will do, and same to yourself, Paddy … Malachy! Get up off that floor and stop giving out.'

The sleet has turned to rain. Paddy makes a dash for the car, and when safely inside he flicks the excess water off the paper before drying it as best he can with the chamois. Then he opens the glove compartment, takes out Grainne's letter and sets it on the passenger seat. He weights it down with the torch he's taken from the boot, shoves the damp police forms into the glove compartment and starts the car. Instead of turning at the bridge he goes in the other direction, down Main Street, and pulls up outside O'Hagan's off-licence. It's closed but Annie O'Hagan is always around till midnight.

He raps the door three times.

'A wee quarter bottle of vodka, Annie, and I'll see you right tomorrow.'

Paddy had settled the last bill only two days ago so he's good for credit. Annie is a crabbit auld thing but she can always be relied on. If there was ever an audition for a female Scrooge, she'd get the part hands down, and she wouldn't need any acting skills either.

'You're a dote, Annie,' Paddy says, giving her one of his most engaging of smiles. He should have saved himself the trouble.

Turning the car round, he drives across the bridge this time, but heads towards the factory where he can pull in and sit for a bit without being seen by too many nosy parkers. The top of the quarter bottle unscrews easily. He's taking his third swig as he pulls into the lane that runs alongside the factory wall. After turning off the engine, and with the bottle lodged safely between his knees, he pulls the letter from under the torch. There are three sheets of crisp Basildon Bond filled with sprawling handwriting. He turns the torch on and reads.

The last drops of vodka are being sucked dry by the time he gets to the third page. Only one sentence on the last sheet, and a signature in a hand showing the effects of the sedatives.

I just want you to know that despite all the bad stuff, you're the nicest man I've ever met and Mairead is lucky to have you.

Grainne

Paddy doesn't feel sick any more. Just tired. So, so tired. He wants to get home. He wants to put his arms around Mairead. He wants her to hold him. And most of all he wants to see his children, tell them things are sorted, tell them nothing like this will ever happen again. Ever.

He takes the last page of the letter and puts it back into the envelope, sliding it under the sheaf of forms in the glove compartment. He gets out of the car, walks a few yards to the end of the wall and, hunkering down, digs a hole in the wet earth with the neck of the empty bottle. Shredding the first two pages of the letter, he lets the pieces fall, mashing them into the clay with the bottle. Only one tiny scrap escapes in a gust of wind.

He covers the hole up with the sole of his shoe and hurls the vodka bottle into the darkness. Then manoeuvring the narrow lane in reverse, he takes the shortcut home.

APRIL
1972

I. Mairead

Mairead has just lit the oven. They're having steak and kidney pies for tea – home-baked, special offer ones from McNamee's, not Fray Bentos. Niamh won't be too pleased about that, nor Eamon either, probably. Well, if they're hungry enough they'll eat what's put in front of them.

The oven will take a good fifteen minutes to heat so she has time to wash a few nappies. Hopefully, this will be her last year of nappies, though if Shauna is lazy like her brothers she'll be wearing them at night for longer than Mairead would like.

She fills the sink with the hot water she has boiled and adds a generous dose of Daz. Then she runs the cold water hard to take the scald off. Dropping the nappies in one by one, she adds a squirt of washing up liquid for good measure. Best to let them soak for a few minutes.

She's filling the kettle again when she catches sight of Niall scampering up the back garden path, the bag of messages swinging. The bag is as big as he is.

'Mammy, there was a whole crowd of boys outside Diver's swearing at the army patrol and I think Kieran's with them. It looked like his jumper anyhow.'

Niall is panting as he puts the fresh baps and pan loaf in the bread bin. Digging into his trouser pocket he gathers the loose change and drops it onto the draining board.

'What do you mean it looked like his jumper? What jumper? What colour was it? Was it Kieran or not?'

The box of matches she is setting back onto the window sill manages to tumble into the soapy water and is half submerged before she can retrieve it.

'I dunno – green, blue, I can't remember,' Niall says. 'Maybe it wasn't Kieran, I dunno. I was scared they were going to start throwing stones so I ran up the back lane to get away from them. The Duffys were there and so was that Donal Maguire one. He was doing the most shouting. When's tea ready?'

For the life of her she can't remember what Kieran is wearing. He had left amidst their usual bickering – him refusing once again to wear Martin Donnelly's hand-me-down bomber jacket and her warning him it was going to rain and he would catch his death.

She dumps the soggy matches on top of the overflowing rubbish bin.

'How many of them were there?' Mairead persists.

'Dunno. Ten maybe. I dunno.'

'Where was the patrol heading?' Keeping the panic out of her voice is difficult.

'Dunno. I told you, I came on home. When's tea ready? I'm starving.'

Niall is fidgeting with his ears, twitching the way he does when he's anxious. He's too sensitive. It's worrying. Paddy insists it's her fault – too much mollycoddling. Perhaps he's right. But it's hard not to feel protective towards Niall. He's small for his age. Children on the street pick on him, call him 'shorty four-eyes'. She's been to Dr Hennessy, had the tests done. He'll grow in his own good time, according to the results. Well, hopefully it'll be sooner than later. Strange thing is, though, Niall never complains. He acts like it doesn't bother him. But of course it bothers him. It can't not bother him.

'Here, have a Rich Tea to keep you going. Actually, take the packet and share them out with the rest of them. It'll be an hour before tea's ready. I have to run a quick message first.' She nods mechanically when Niall pushes for two biscuits.

Stepping over Shauna, who is on the floor playing with an old tea set of Niamh's, she goes into the living room as Niall heads out to the Green where the other four are playing cricket. Thank God the weather has stayed dry or she'd be tortured with them indoors. She looks out the front window just in time to see Sinead snatch the packet of biscuits from Niall. Mairead slides her fingers through the slats on the venetian blinds to open the window.

'Sinead, can you come in here please.' Her voice is shriller than intended.

Sinead knows better than to ignore her. And she's smart enough to hand the packet back to her brother immediately, though not before grabbing her share.

Shauna has crawled her way over to Mairead's leg and is using it for support to pull herself up before grabbing hold of a chair leg. None of them took this long to walk. It's pure laziness; Shauna's too used to being lifted and laid like a doll by the whole lot of them. No wonder she's a pudding.

'Oh, did she take another step?' Sinead says, blustering in and going straight over to Shauna. 'Come on, Shauna, walk to Sinead. Come on, come on … that's it, you can do it.'

'Sinead, don't think I didn't see that. What have I told you about being a bully?'

'What? I didn't do anything.'

Mairead has no time to get into an argument.

'Listen, I have to go to Diver's. Keep an eye on the baby until I get back.'

'But it's my innings next. Why can't Niamh do it?'

'You're lucky I don't keep you in for the rest of the day so do as you're told.'

Mairead doesn't wait for a retort. She's already pulled Paddy's fishing anorak from the cubbyhole under the stairs and is heading for the scullery where she turns down the oven. Scooping up the coins from the draining board, she heads out the back way.

The crunch of gravel under her feet is the only sound in the lane along the back of the houses. But as she nears the turning that converges with the next estate, Rita Donoghue's distinctive voice is carrying over the high hedge of the end houses in Drummore Court. There's more than the usual tone of urgent gossip in her words, and as Rita's plump figure comes into focus so does the nature of the monologue she's delivering to Jim Quigley and his wife, Anne.

'It's wile altogether, that's what it is. You'd think they'd nothing better to do than be lifting youngsters. Sure they're only a lock of wains acting the hard men. Mind you, half of them soldiers is wains themselves.'

Mairead is in two minds whether to pretend she hasn't

noticed anyone there. She wants to get to Diver's as quickly as possible. Curiosity gets the better of her and she approaches the group reluctantly.

'Ach hello there, Mairead. Did you hear about the commotion down the Ballybeehan Road? I missed it by a hair's breath, but Nora Diver heard all about it from Gerry Devine.'

Jim and Anne Quigley say hello and goodbye before Mairead has the chance to form a response, which is just as well because the air in her windpipe is caught. By the time Rita has relayed more third-hand details, no doubt heavily embellished, Mairead has regained her composure. She should have known better than to stop. It's pointless enquiring about who the boys were. Rita Donoghue is one of those women who has little or no significant information to impart about anything or anyone, ever. Unfortunately, Rita herself has no awareness of this, so she goes about undeterred in her mission to regurgitate old news to anyone who has the time and patience to listen. And Mairead has neither one nor the other at this particular moment.

'It's desperate, Rita. I don't know what things are coming to. How's Patrick doing?' Mairead asks, stepping down off the footpath in preparation for her escape.

Patrick Donoghue is on benefits after the mildest of strokes and there's no sign of him going back to work. And why should he? Isn't he and half the town better off with all the allowances they're getting at the taxpayer's expense? Mairead lowers her eyes. Cynicism: not a trait she's proud of; Rita and Patrick Donoghue haven't a bad bone in their bodies.

'Aw Mairead, he'll never be the man he was. He's to be pitied, so he is.'

Yeah, Rita, try telling that to the Dole Man if he catches him with a pint of Guinness in his hand.

'Sorry, Rita, I'm in a mad rush to get the tea on. You know what they're like when they're hungry,' she says, faking a businesslike burst of energy.

'Oh aye, I know too well. Away you go, Mairead. Don't be letting me keep you back.'

When Mairead arrives at Diver's there's not a soul to be seen outside, and the shop itself has only one customer – Philomena Lafferty. Nora Diver is excitedly relating the incident.

The two women pause and acknowledge Mairead's presence. Then Nora responds to a question Philomena has just asked.

'No, the patrol was heading back down the Ballybeehan Road when the boys appeared out of nowhere. According to Gerry Devine there was a lot of goading going on and stones were thrown. There was a Saracen parked at the bottom of the bray. Most of the boys escaped through the barbed-wire fence and ran across Duggan's field. I saw nothing myself cause the shop was busy.'

Mairead casually joins in the conversation. 'God Almighty, when is it ever going to end?'

If Nora Diver knew Kieran was among them she would have said so by now. Mrs Lafferty has already lost interest so she opens her purse and pays, leaving Mrs Diver free to start the story all over again.

'It's madness, so it is. Gerry Devine said that …'

As it turns out, Rita Donoghue had already passed on whatever information there was to be had and so now Mairead is eager to get away. Two children come into the shop and Mairead takes the opportunity to end the conversation when Nora gets distracted. No one will ever get away with nicking when Nora Diver is manning the shop.

'A box of matches there, Nora.' Mairead hands over a 10p coin. She needs the change to call Paddy. Where in the name of God is Kieran?

The telephone box in Clonleigh Crescent is closer than the one at the bottom of Drummore Court. She squeezes the 2p coin into the slot the minute the pips go.

'Can I speak to Paddy Reilly, please. It's his wife.'

'Aye, could you hold on there a wee minute.'

She doesn't recognise the voice on the other end of the line.

'Paddy, it's your missus on the phone for you.'

It seems like ages before Paddy lifts the phone.

'Mairead?'

'Paddy, listen, I don't know what to do,' she blurts out, and then attempts as succinctly and coherently as possible to tell him everything that's happened.

'Mairead, are you not overreacting a bit? You know what Niall is like for telling tall tales.'

'No, it wasn't like that. I know when he's exaggerating. He was scared, and I know by the way he was talking that he's sure it was Kieran. What if he's been lifted, Paddy? You need to do something – go over to the barracks or whatever place it is they take those boys they're going to interrogate. What if he gets interned?'

'No one's going to be interned. Are you even sure anyone's been lifted?'

Mairead can't answer. Of course, she isn't flamin' sure. Paddy's standard response to hearsay: if you don't witness something with your own two eyes, you can't be going about drawing conclusions.

'Are you still there, Mairead?'

'Yes, I'm still here.'

The pips start going. She goes to insert another coin but changes her mind.

What did she expect? He'd tried to hide it but she could hear him rolling his eyes, maybe looking at the clock, more concerned about collecting dockets for the next race, trying to be patient with her characteristic tendency for histrionics in all things pertaining to the Troubles. In fairness, it's not as if she's got a whole lot to go on. Why hadn't she checked Kieran's jumpers upstairs before she left? How stupid was that? All the same, Paddy could have been a bit more supportive.

She leaves the telephone box and heads up home.

How can she get him to see that Kieran is in danger? It's not her imagination. Paddy was there when Sinead told them about the way Kieran stood up to the soldiers. It might have appeared brave to Sinead, but Mairead was shocked that Kieran could come out with such aggressive statements. Paddy, on the other hand, took it in his stride, said Kieran didn't say anything he shouldn't have. Maybe so, but that's not the point, is it? Look what happened on Bloody Sunday. Young boys like Kieran with no sense repeating what they hear on the TV. This is the British army we're talking about. They think they're fighting a war, that's their job; they're only following orders. Nobody will be stopping them from shooting more young boys if that's what they're told to do.

And Kieran is far too old for his age. He might give someone the wrong impression. Lately, he's been coming out with the weirdest things he's read in books, like 'I cannot believe in a God who wants to be praised at all times', or 'Is man merely a mistake of God's? Or God merely a mistake of man's?' Some of his grand quotations border on blasphemy, so they do. But she has to remember it's his age. Apparently it's normal to question things. That doesn't mean it's not embarrassing sometimes. Mairead dreads it when people visit in case he gets into a discussion with them. He drives Sinead and Niamh mad when he needs an audience. Well, more Sinead. Only yesterday they had a huge fight about faith.

'I'll tell you what faith is, Sinead. It's you not wanting to know what the truth is, that's all.'

Sinead can hold her own with the best of them, but Kieran's nonsense gets her flustered, mainly because it sounds so clever. And of course Sinead's too stubborn to admit she doesn't know the meanings of half the fancy words he uses – *no one* understands what Kieran's going on about half the time. But Mairead would rather have this phase than when he was going through the seizures. Thank God that's over.

It has started to drizzle. No hood on the coat and her with her lovely hair permed and set by Moira only two days ago. It'll be a frizz by the time she gets home. She quickens her step but has to slow it down. The soles of her worn-out shoes have no grip. They're for the bin as soon as this month's pay comes in. The minute she reaches the gravelled lane she practically runs home, though there's probably no saving her hairdo.

All the children except Kieran are gathered in the living room.

'Mammy, what took you so long? We're starving.'

'Stop your complaining. Tea'll be ready in ten minutes.'

Twenty is closer to the truth but white lies invariably placate hungry bellies, providing you don't veer too far off the mark.

'Is Kieran not back yet?' Mairead asks after the pies are in the oven.

'He's upstairs,' Sinead answers.

Mairead throws the anorak back into the cubbyhole and climbs the stairs. Kieran's feet are in view through the gap in the half-closed door. He appears to be stretched out on the bed. What has she told them about lying on the bed with their shoes on? She's about to fling the door open but instead goes into her own room to check her hair in the mirror and catch her breath. Outside, the drizzle has picked up pace. The Green looks dismal, abandoned, but for the makeshift wicket standing stark and forlorn.

She closes the blinds and turns on the light. Her reflection is as grey as the daylight but her hair has withstood the onslaught. Reaching for her lipstick, she juts her face towards the mirror. Lipstick never fails to liven up even the most unfortunate of faces. She needs a new colour though. This 'Mother's Pink', as the girls call it, is too bland now, especially in the winter. A red would be better. Moira wears red and you barely notice the smoker's lines etched on her upper lip.

Mairead strains closer to the mirror. Is it the light or are those permanent wrinkles forming on her cheeks? She pulls her lips taut across her teeth in a fake smile, then releases them. Impossible. She repeats the grimace, more intense this time, changing the angle of her face. The lines disappear. It was the light.

The sound of Kieran's footsteps on the stairs puts the lipstick back in its place. She fluffs the curls on the crown of her head and twists her fringe into place. Before going downstairs she goes into the boys' room and takes a look around. Nothing out of the ordinary beyond the rumpled bed and a couple of books strewn on the floor.

In the living room they're watching Doctor Who — except for Kieran who's sitting at the table, trying to give the impression he's outgrown Doctor Who, as well as a whole pile of other things. He can fool himself but he can't fool her. No harm in it really, except when he might think he's so grown up he can join the IRA, a desire he has never actually expressed in words, if she's honest. Still, she's no doubt it's crossed his mind. Her stomach somersaults at the thought of it, catapulting her back into reality. The IRA is getting stronger by the day according to Mickey Donnelly, who hasn't stopped ranting since Bloody Sunday.

'They're queuing up to join the Provos after what happened in Derry,' he'd informed Mairead when she popped in to return Eileen's garden shears.

Where does Mickey get his information from, that's what Mairead would like to know? And it's not as if Mickey has any staunch beliefs or has anything to do with the IRA. He's far too cowardly, as are all Eileen's boys — scared of their own shadows. Wasn't it Kieran who stood up to the British army during the raid and not Martin Donnelly? The apple doesn't fall too far from the tree, that's for sure. Did either Eileen or Gerard Donnelly come rushing across the Green to see why an army Saracen was parked outside? No, of course they didn't. And Eileen knew full well the children were home alone. She might have flapped about afterwards, letting on she'd heard nothing the whole time the raid was taking place, but she was quick enough to land when the Saracen pulled out of the estate, wasn't she?

Niamh lets out a squeal at the daleks. Mairead goes over to the fire and throws on a lock of coal. One of the pieces rolls to the front and lodges itself dangerously close to the edge. Unable to coax it back with the poker she grabs it like she would a hot potato and drops into a space at the back of the grate.

'You'd think one of you boys would have the sense to keep the fire going. You're getting as lazy as sin.'

'Sorry, Mammy,' Niall says. 'Is the tea nearly ready?'

Mairead ignores him, glancing at Kieran on her way to the scullery.

'Where were you all day, Kieran?'

'Over at the football pitch watching a match.'

'Oh, right.'

She goes on into the scullery. Is Kieran a bit more subdued than usual? Probably not. One thing's for sure though – Mairead is more than glad to see he's wearing his Aran sweater. Not a trace of green to be seen.

She almost smiles as she takes the nappies from the cold water and drops them into a basin to be rewashed after tea. For once there's comfort in Paddy being right. She'll have to get to grips with this paranoia. Her mother is no help, ranting on all the time about history repeating itself. Maybe the fog will lift with this Widgery investigation. The government will come to their senses, abolish internment. There's bound to be peace after that. Sure if they agree to treat everyone the same, things can get back to normal. Who could have imagined the Troubles would last this long? It's pure madness.

The pies are browning nicely. Five more minutes. Doctor Who will be over any minute now. She hurries to open the last two tins of beans and empties them into a frying pan. The sauce thickens quicker that way. None of them likes their beans runny. When the tea is brewed and the bread buttered, she turns off the oven and reaches up to the press for the plates.

'Can someone set the table, please?'

The usual squabbling starts up. In the end it's less hassle if she does it herself.

By the time she gets Shauna fed, checking that Eamon and Michael aren't making too much of a mess, the big ones have cleaned their plates, thankfully without too much grumbling about the pies. When Paddy walks in she's already steeped the plates and is mopping up the sauce in the frying pan with a half slice of bread. She'll make herself some toast later. Normally, there are leftovers but not this evening.

'False alarm, Paddy, sorry. I don't know what got into me, honestly,' she half whispers, taking his pie and beans from the oven.

'Where did you get your information from anyhow? Like an idiot I called at the barracks on the way back and they didn't have a baldy what I was on about.'

Mairead can't help laughing. Paddy is sort of laughing too.

'You'll have us both in the grave with this fixation about Kieran taking up the gun to fight for The Cause,' Paddy says. 'I could see through it if we came from a Nationalist background – and your mother doesn't count. Singing a few songs about the Easter Rising of 1916 doesn't qualify her as a rebel. You might be able to take her seriously if she had half a note in her head.'

'Don't be cruel,' Mairead scolds half-heartedly.

When Paddy's in good form, there's no one this side of the county who can match his humour.

'Tea or milk?' she asks.

'A cup of tea will do,' he says lifting his plate. 'No bread, though. I'm not that hungry'

When Paddy brings his empty plate back into the scullery, Mairead is drying the last of the knives and forks and putting them in the drawer.

'Do you fancy going to Malloy's for an hour later on?' Paddy asks. 'There's a wee band playing and Leo gave me a couple of free tickets.'

Mairead hesitates. Lately she's been finding any excuse not to go out. It isn't just the money. It's also that she's put on weight and nothing fits her.

'We don't have to stay long,' Paddy coaxes.

It's obvious he's keen to go. If she refuses, he won't object. He's been trying so hard to turn over a new leaf, which is why even if she allows him, he won't agree to going on his own. She doesn't want to disappoint him. She'll find something to wear. She's had her hair done, after all, so with a bit of make-up she'll pass herself.

'We'll have to be there a bit early if we want to get a table. I'll get the wee ones bathed. That'll give you more time to get ready,' Paddy says, heading for the bathroom. 'Right, you lot, bath time. Off with the rags!' he calls out.

Mairead goes to the living room, gets clean underwear and pyjamas from the hot press, and lays them on the arm of the couch before undressing Shauna.

'Come on, you heard what Daddy said!'

Eamon and Michael stop what they're doing and start taking off their clothes. When Paddy lifts Shauna and marches the boys off like soldiers, Mairead sits down. It'll be fine. A couple of Babychams won't break the bank. Paddy only drinks the odd shandy. All that worrying about his drinking for nothing. And she doesn't have to get up to dance if she doesn't want to. Paddy won't mind.

The box of cigarettes is less than half full. Eight to be

precise. If she smokes one now she'll have enough to get through the evening and won't need to buy another packet until after Mass tomorrow. In fact, she might not even buy another packet at all. She's tried it the other way, weaning herself off them; it doesn't work. Cold turkey is the best option – everyone says so, and there's no time like the present. There. Proof of the pudding she's ready to give them up – she can't be bothered finishing the one she's just lit up. Nicking it, she puts it back in the packet. With the money she saves from giving up she'll be able to afford a new outfit.

Images of a new dress and the blazing fire lull her into a half doze, which is broken abruptly when Shauna climbs on to her lap smelling like a soap commercial.

'Dummy, Mammy!'

'Not until you're in bed.'

She looks at the clock. Half past seven already.

'I'm away in for a shave. Then I have to call for a bit with Eileen. We'll leave at about nine, okay?' Paddy says, bustling off.

Mairead nods, still drowsy.

Climbing the stairs with Shauna in her arms and the two boys ahead of her, she rubs her forehead in a vain attempt to fight off a migraine that's beginning to surface.

'Get your prayers said and then straight into bed,' she tells the boys as she goes into the girls' room. She draws the curtains before handing Shauna her dummy and tucking her into the cot. Shauna is far too big to be sleeping in a cot. They'll have to get rid of the double bed and put in two sets of single bunks. It's been nagging at Mairead for weeks. She should put any notions of new clothes out of her head.

'Eamon, will you please get into the bed properly,' she scolds when she goes into the boys' room.

He's tucked himself in at the bottom end of the bed.

'But Michael is farting, Mammy.'

Mairead is having none of his nonsense and pulls the blankets up for him to get out.

After they have settled down, facing away from each other, she checks that the plastic sheet's in place. When will the bed-wetting stop? Drying sheets in front of the fire is an everyday occurrence some weeks in the winter. Cajoling, shouting, slapping – nothing works. Not even promises of chocolate. She goes to the bottom of the bed to where the blankets have been pulled out by Eamon. She hates the corners of blankets dangling untidily on a bed. And besides, cold air can creep in during the night and freeze your toes.

She needs to hurry it up if she wants to get her make-up on without it being a last minute job, and she still hasn't figured out what she's going to wear. If only she could get out of it.

Lifting the mattress irritably, she tries to tuck and smooth out the satin-trimmed corners underneath while being careful not to scratch her hand on any of the springs that have come loose on the bed itself. But when she drops the mattress it doesn't sit as it should on the iron frame, which means the blankets have bundled up. Goddamn it.

With more force, she raises the mattress off the frame again, higher than before.

'Mammy, what are you doing?'

'Lie down, Michael,' she snaps as she strains to get both arms well under the mattress.

Her left hand brushes against a softness that doesn't belong to the blanket. She abandons her efforts to smooth and tuck at loose sheets and satin borders.

The boys are still, like the air in the room, and the hall light through the half-closed door affords no more than a soft glow in the semi-darkness. But there's no mistaking the unravelling threads of wool, squirming like worms around a hole in the royal blue striped jumper she has dragged out from under the mattress.

II. Sinead

'I'M TRYING, SINEAD, but my eyes just won't stay closed.'

Enough is enough. I can't stand it any more.

'Niamh, I'm knackered. For the hundredth time, you are not going to die in your sleep.' I'm scream-whispering at her and spit is flying all over her face. Serves her right. 'When has a bomb ever gone off in the middle of the night? Can you answer me that? Can you?'

Okay, so I'm bluffing a bit. But what else can I do? She's driving me bananas.

'Stop spitting. And your breath is disgusting,' Niamh scream-whispers back at me.

We're in Granny's and we've been lying in the dark for hours again. It'll be daylight soon, which is when we finally managed to doze off last night, and the night before, and the night before that. Even if a bomb does go off there's always a warning. But there's no point trying to tell Niamh that. I feel like giving her a slap. She needs to wise up and grow up.

And if she thinks she's going to sneak her way out of living with Granny on her own like I've had to do, then she's got another think coming.

I'm not saying she's faking – she really is scared of the IRA – but the agreement was that she'd do half the days when she started the grammar school and I'd only have to keep her company for a bit in the beginning. Until she got used to it.

Obviously no sign of that happening.

Far too much fuss, if you ask me.

There was none of this when I got landed with it. I was simply told that someone had to go live with Granny after Aunty Moira got married. I know it's only at the other end of town but it felt like I'd been sent to boarding school. I'd cried and cried at the end of that first weekend home. 'Please, please Mammy, it's lonely. I want to stay home.'

Fat lot of good it did.

Granny is a dote and we get on the best but she doesn't even have a television. Nor an inside loo. Having to pee in a pot during the night is one thing I'll never get used to. And it's an even bigger problem when there's two of us. Like now.

'Can you not just hold on to it, Niamh? The smell makes me sick.'

But no, up she gets – again.

I don't hear any dribbles.

'Get back into bed, will you?'

'It's coming … I have to do a number two as well,' she snaps.

Cheeky bitch.

'Don't you dare, Niamh, I'm warning you. Get back into bed this very minute.'

My extra-cross voice always works. I get a strong whiff of the pee as she pushes the pot back under my side of the bed and clamours over the top of me. That's another problem – Niamh has to be by the wall. Why? Wait for it … ever since she fell out of bed one night, she's convinced that ghosts exist. She actually believes that a hand came from under the bed and pulled her down on to the floor. So I have to sleep on the outside now.

'No more talking.'

I'm crossing my fingers under the blankets, trying not to move a muscle.

I might pretend to be sick in the morning. We have English first thing and I haven't done my homework. Knowing my luck Miss Logan will check me. Plus I can't find my apron and headband for Domestic Science. Again.

'Sinead, are you awake?'

She's moving closer to me.

'Sinead … SINEAD …'

'Bloody hell, Niamh, would you just go to sleep. For fuck's sake …'

'Did you just say the eff word? I don't believe you just said the eff word! You can swear all you like, Sinead, but I'm telling you that the IRA could get it mixed up and think the Johnsons live here.'

'I keep telling you that even if they did get mixed up, the IRA don't go into houses and shoot innocent people just because they're Protestants.'

That's the end of it. I'm going to ignore her. No matter what. It's Friday tomorrow so we'll be back home. Mammy and Daddy will have to sort this out because I'm not coming back down on Monday. Unless things at home are still the same as they were last Sunday evening when me and Niamh left.

In that case, I'd rather stay at Granny's.

The fighting started on Saturday evening when Mammy went into a hysterical fit because she thought Kieran had been throwing stones at the army even though Kieran said he wasn't. Daddy could do nothing to calm her down, and then she started calling Daddy 'irresponsible' and other things I know she probably didn't mean. Kieran stomped off to his room and refused to say anything more, which only made Mammy twice as paranoid about Kieran ending up in the IRA. Anyway, Daddy had given up trying to talk any sense into her when she started going on about St Columb's boarding school. Daddy looked at her like she was a woman possessed and told her to get a grip of herself, at which point Mammy completely lost it and screamed in Daddy's face, 'If I have to beg, steal or borrow, he's going to St Columb's and that's that, Paddy!' Daddy had gritted his teeth and grabbed his jacket. 'Over my dead body,' he shouted back at her. 'I'm not going to listen to this insanity one minute longer.' Then he stormed out, nearly taking the hinges off the front door.

All the next day it was like morgue in our house. Daddy stayed away, Kieran wasn't allowed out of his room except to eat, and Mammy spent practically all day in the scullery smoking. In the end, it was a relief to get down to Granny's.

The thing is, I'm so tired of Kieran and his problems. Okay, the petit mal wasn't his fault, but all this constant worry about whether or not he'll end up fighting for The Cause is driving me nuts. I don't know how much more of it I can stand. The rest of us have got plenty of things Mammy should be worrying about. Like the fact that I'm probably the only girl in my class who doesn't wear a bra yet. Or has a period. Maybe I don't have proper breasts but that doesn't mean I can't wear a bra, for Pete's sake. God forbid anyone in this family can have problems compared to Kieran's. It's not one bit fair. Actually I don't care whether or not they're still acting like lunatics when I go home tomorrow. I'm going to sort out this Granny situation once and for all. And they better not try to bring Niamh's eye problem into it either – she's been fine for ages now.

Imagine, two months of green puss in her eyes and nothing the matter with her? Nothing. As soon as the eye specialist told her it was 'psychosomatic' it stopped. Just like that. Abracadabra, no more puss. Would you believe it? In one way, though, her being psychosomatic for a while was grand because I kept getting called to the Reverend Mother's office to take Niamh home when her eyelashes got stuck together. It was disgusting. I did feel a bit sorry for her. No wonder she hasn't made any friends, though I don't think it's only the gooey eyes that have made her unpopular. Her being a cheat hasn't done much to help.

The truth is, Niamh's not great at remembering stuff and when two girls in her class caught her with the map of Ireland drawn on her arm, she was sent to Coventry. She came running to me in hysterics when it happened and although I ate the face off her for being an eejit and a cheat, I have to say I was impressed. That was some map she'd drawn. All thirty-two counties, with Derry on her wrist and Cork in the crook of her arm. It must have taken her ages.

Hallelujah, she's asleep. Finally.

I wonder if Granny will make us bacon butties for breakfast? My tummy's beginning to rumble now. What time is it? The Timex Aunty Moira bought me when I failed the 11-Plus is broken and I'm lost without it.

Granny gets up every morning after six to get the stove going and the fire lit. I'm going to miss her baking and cooking … her soda farls … her treacle bread … her fried steak and gravy and … Oh, I must have dozed off. There's rattling going on in the scullery now.

No smell of bacon though.

I don't want bacon butties anyway. Thick slices of treacle bread with butter and blackberry jam …

Damn it, Niamh. I can't believe she's pushed the pot back under the bed at exactly the point I'd left my shoes. If there's as much as a drop spilt, I'll kill her. I swear to God, I will. And I don't care if I'm the first to go down the yard – I'm leaving the pot for Niamh to empty. She may as well get used to it. I've a good mind to wake her up.

The scullery door is shut tight but there's a lovely smell of turf in the living room. I scoot out the back hall, grab the torch and nearly fall flat on my face trying to hurry to the toilet. It's a good job my brogues have brilliant grip. I'm in and out like a flash because there's no way I'm going to wash my hands in freezing water.

'Sinead, pet, you need to watch yourself on those slabs. You're up early! Are you ready for your breakfast?' Granny has the table already set.

'I'm starving.'

She's putting the cosy on the tea pot that's sitting by the fire. Her blouse is inside out, again. And she's got a pair of sandals on.

We think Granny is beginning to dote. I mean, a few weeks back, when I poured the tea for supper there was nothing but boiled water in the pot. We had a bit of a laugh about it, but then she forgot to use Bisto for the gravy a couple of days later and insisted that she never uses Bisto to make gravy. Granny has a sharp tongue on her when the notion takes her, so I ended up having to eat the watery, tasteless stock that should have had a bit of Bisto in it. But I told Mammy about it. She's noticed a few things herself and thinks Granny could have a bit of senile dementia, which happens to lots of old people. The thing is, my granny might be seventy-two but she doesn't look it and she's as fit as a fiddle. Sometimes I go to the chapel with her to light a candle and I can barely keep up with her. Granny doesn't walk, she marches.

'Turn the wireless up a wee bit, pet.'

Granny couldn't manage without four things: Mass, *The Messenger*, her wireless and *The Irish News*, which she sends every week to Uncle Sean in England. The wireless is on nearly non-stop and you daren't speak when it's time for the News or the Angelus. These last months, especially, she has been obsessed with the news because of what happened in Derry on Bloody Sunday. And to think Kieran and Daddy nearly ended up going. Wasn't it lucky Mammy went ballistic even though Daddy tried to explain to her it was a 'peaceful civil rights demonstration against internment and it was everyone's moral duty to go'?

Anyway, Granny has been going on for two months about how it's not the first time it's happened and nothing will ever change and the Bee Specials and the Paratroopers are just different names for the Black and Tans. She must have explained this to me a million times but I still can't figure out what these Bee Specials are. Or the Black and Tans that were around in her day and which she never shuts up about.

Yes, that's right, my granny is a bit of a rebel. But only because she lived through the 1916 Uprising and had a cousin who was in Croke Park in 1920 when the police started shooting into the crowd. They called that Bloody Sunday too, according to Granny. I thought she was making it up until I asked the history teacher, who told me there was a Bloody Sunday in 1920, and another one in 1913, and it wasn't as simple as the British government killing innocent people like Granny would have you believe. Mrs O'Kane should know, her being a history teacher and all, even if most of the stuff we have to learn is about the British Empire.

Granny has never said so, but I've a feeling her cousin was in the IRA. I wouldn't be surprised if Granny herself had been a 'Freedom Fighter'. She does go on and on about the likes of Kevin Barry. Don't get me wrong though. She's great at telling a story, and in the beginning I loved hearing about Eamon de Valera and Michael Collins and all the other stuff. But it can get a bit boring after a while. Plus she might, just might, be a teeny-weeny bit of a bigot. I mean, she's still not really on the best of terms with Aunty Moira because she married a Protestant. It's ludicrous. Just because he's not Catholic. Sure didn't he agree to get married in a Catholic church and have their future children baptised Catholic? What more does Granny want? I'm dying dead about Uncle George, and I love it when we go to Coleraine, especially when the Twelfth of July parades are on.

Anyway, the problem is that since Bloody Sunday Granny has been on a rant about 'a United Ireland' and 'an Ireland divided will never be at peace'. I let her rant because of the dementia and I feel sorry for her, but there are times I wish she'd just stop. I mean, the Troubles have been going on for too long. What was wrong with the way things were? Though I can hardly remember what things were like before any more, and half the time when Granny is telling her stories I get lost because she jumps from the past to the present in between sentences. I'm not saying people shouldn't stand up for themselves – or as Kieran, being

Kieran, would put it, 'be true to their social conscience' – but for God Almighty's sake, is it better to be blowing shops up and killing people? You'd think we were in the middle of World War Three. Honestly, the whole thing's getting ridiculous.

Things have got worse since Tuesday. This Lord Widgery character has published some sort of report and Granny has been on an even bigger rant, if that's possible. If I have to hear the phrase 'never trust a man in a wig' one more time …

'Granny, is there any treacle bread and blackberry jam left over from yesterday?'

I asked her this question ten minutes ago but she brought me a plate of soda bread instead. I didn't like to tell her I wasn't actually in the mood for soda bread so I ate two bits without jam. She's about to answer when Niamh comes clumping down the stairs with her hair standing on the top of her head. She looks like one of Fagin's orphans.

'Where's the pot, Niamh?' I ask.

'Oops, I forgot it,' she answers.

'I'll do it later, pet,' Granny pipes up, lifting the teapot and pouring Niamh a cup. Niamh is a sneaky drawers. She might be able to fool Granny but she can't fool me.

'Are you sure, Granny?' she says, standing on the bottom stair like butter wouldn't melt in her mouth.

As if she's any intention of going back up for it. Oh, I could whack her. She sits down at the table and grabs a soda farl.

'That's far too much butter you're putting on,' I tell her.

Then Granny brings out a small plate with two pieces of treacle bread and a half-empty jar of jam. I grab them both before Niamh can. She's got no manners whatsoever.

'I asked for the treacle bread, Niamh. You have a whole soda farl in front of you, so don't be so greedy, all right?' I lift my knife to spread the butter.

Niamh quickly gulps down some tea and has her mouth half open to complain to Granny when the music for the eight o'clock news starts.

'Whist,' Granny says and I look at Niamh, my eyebrows up where they should be.

'Yes, Niamh, whist would you.'

'Turn the sound up there, Sinead,' Granny says, sitting down on the armchair nearest the table. I wonder if going deaf is part of senile dementia. I've already turned the volume up and can hardly hear myself think as it is. Niamh is grinding her teeth and giving me filthy looks as the headlines come on, all dramatic.

'March organiser and MP Ivan Cooper ... Westminster parliament ... Edward Heath ... tribunal ... Lord Chief Justice Lord Widgery ...'

I take a big juicy bite of my treacle bread, close my eyes to show how delicious it is, and then smack my lips good and loud – Niamh is *so* easy to wind up. I'm getting ready to sink my teeth in again when I look over at Niamh, expecting to see her cheeks blazing. Instead, she's gone as pale as a ghost and is staring at Granny.

'It'll be all out war after this,' Granny is saying for the hundredth time this week as she gets up off the armchair and lifts the teapot from the table.

'What do you mean *it'll be all out war?*' Niamh asks.

I've explained to Niamh about Granny beginning to dote, and if I've told her once I have told her a million times to ignore half of what Granny comes out with. She usually keeps dead quiet when Granny gets going. So what's she doing now, asking such a silly question?

'The IRA won't be taking this sitting down, and rightly so too. I'm not one for fighting, pet, but who's going to defend the Irish Catholics of Northern Ireland if it's not going to be the IRA? Not the Queen's Militia that's for sure.'

What has Granny got against the royal family? She's always knocking them. What have they got to do with anything, for Pete's sake?

'I'll make us a fresh pot,' Granny says, heading for the scullery. But she's gone all stiff and angry and her cheeks are blazing.

Niamh has stopped eating her soda bread. After only one bite.

'Ach, what have I told you? Pay no attention to Granny,' I whisper to Niamh.

She's staring at her soda farl like a zombie.

'Here, I was only joking. You can have the other piece of treacle bread. I'm full up. Do you want jam on it?'

'No, thanks, I'm not hungry.'

She gets up from the table.

'I'm going to get ready for school,' she says, walking towards the staircase.

'But you've hardly eaten anything, Niamh. You'll get sick.'

'I won't get sick, I'll be fine,' she says, and climbs the stairs.

III. Paddy

'Jesus, Mairead, what's it going to take for you to trust your own son?'

After a week of silence he's decided to take the bull by the horns. Literally.

'He's lying, Paddy. That jumper did not get torn on the branch of any bloody tree. He was there with those boys. That tear is from barbed wire. Neither you nor anyone else is going to tell me different.'

She storms past armed with a brittle aggression that almost topples him. How's a man expected to be patient when faced with the likes of this?

'That's your problem,' he shouts, standing his ground. 'You're a law onto yourself. You get stuck in your paranoia. Get an appointment with Dr Hennessy before you do all our heads in with your nonsense.'

'You're the one needs to see a bloody doctor, Paddy, not me. If you were ever at home or spent any time with Kieran you might be able to see he's scared and lying through his teeth.'

His palm comes down on the table with far less impact than he'd intended. More of a smack than a slam.

'I hold down three jobs to keep this family,' he manages to croak. Saliva has a way of sabotaging him when he's agitated.

'Yeah, so you keep saying. Well, I hold down seven jobs. How about that?'

The words are precisely pitched to obliterate his coughing and spluttering.

'I said it before and I'll say it again, he'll be going to no bloody boarding school, so just get that notion out of your head,' he roars at the living room door.

She's marching upstairs.

'We'll see about that come September,' she lashes back at him.

The statement hangs for a split second before charging down the stairs to batter the last bit of bravado out of him.

This is one of those times when he becomes a blustering fool in the face of Mairead's anger. But bluster won't do much to keep Kieran out of St Columb's College. She hasn't a bloody clue what it's like. Kieran will crack. And St Columb's is no place for cry babies.

Paddy hoists himself out of the armchair with what feel like the limbs of a man twice his age. Exhaustion has settled in the cavities of his bones. Maybe he's seriously ill. He could be dead this time next week. He could be dead tomorrow for that matter. Has she ever thought of that? He'd like to see how she'd manage on a teacher's pension. She has a nerve ranting about anything. There's more than one woman he can think of who'd take her place at the blink of an eye. Maybe he should have listened to his mother after all.

'Mairead is a wee bit too heavily endowed with airs and graces, son.' His mother's exact words when he told her he was planning to propose. 'It's not as if she's got anything to have airs and graces about, if you think about it. She's as poor as a church mouse. I'm only saying, son, even though I know it's not my place.'

Airs and graces. Women notice these things.

He adjusts the slats of the blinds to let more light in. The evening sun has cast its last rays on their front lawn. Council negligence has turned the Green into a haven for the children's war games. The wooden makeshift rifles and plastic water pistols appear and disappear from behind the long blades. Michael's blonde head is running for cover. But a shot sends him flailing and staggering to his death. Eamon is standing at a distance, arms in a determined fold. No doubt another squabble with Michael. When is Eamon going to toughen up? Pity he wasn't more like his brother in that department. Maybe if he'd even half an interest in sports they'd get on better. God didn't get the balance right when he produced these two. It's not always easy to be sympathetic towards Eamon. Even the girls don't whine as much as he does. But that doesn't mean Paddy shows favouritism, as Mairead would like everyone to believe.

His eyes land on the other side of the Green where Eileen is leaning against the frame of her front door talking to Sinead and Geraldine. He shouldn't have snapped at Sinead earlier. But he can't deal with her moaning. Surely, at this stage she's old enough to appreciate that she's very fortunate. She doesn't know what problems are. Look at poor Geraldine, back home almost a month now, two stone lighter and weighed down by grief after losing her ten-month-old son. Even the IRA has taken pity on her. She's been punished enough, though there are moments when Paddy is overcome by the strongest feeling that Geraldine would have welcomed the tarring and feathering, that it was part of the reason she came home. What a mess.

Is it possible that Kieran might be caught up in the madness too?

Suddenly Kieran appears beside him out of nowhere.

'Speak of the devil.' The words are out before Paddy can pull them back.

'Well, if I'm the devil, she's the banshee.'

'Don't be cheeky, Kieran.'

'What do you expect? She's a madwoman, so she is. Can't you tell her to just leave me alone?'

'Don't talk about your mother like that, do you hear me?'

'Like what, Da? Like what? I'm not a fuckin' wain any more, in case you hadn't noticed.'

The profanity boots Paddy in the gut. He's never heard Kieran swear before. Could Mairead be right about any of this?

'What did you just say?'

Paddy has come within an inch of Kieran, who backs away, palms raised.

'Sorry, sorry. It just came out. I didn't mean it.'

Their eyes lock. Kieran's head flops to his chest in a matter of seconds.

'Right, you come with me,' Paddy snaps, tearing his jacket from the back of a dining chair and snatching the car key. 'We're going to sort this nonsense out once and for all. It's about time someone started to listen to me around here.'

'Where are we going? I've a football match—'

'Forget it. This is more important.'

'But—'

'Did you not hear what I just said? Now let's go. Move it!'

Upstairs the creak of floorboards on the landing heralds the retreat of Mairead's footsteps into the back bedroom. Can a man not have a private moment with his own bloody son?

'Where are we going?' Kieran asks again. No defiance now.

Paddy has no idea where to go with Kieran. What he does know is he needs time to find some composure.

Castlefin. That's where they'll go. The distance and the silence will steady his breathing.

Red sky at night, shepherd's delight. The horizon is on fire. Who comes up with these silly sayings – as if a red sky at night means anything in Ireland. For every promise of the sun there's a cloud in waiting, ready to hijack.

The sharp turn into the country road nearly lands him in a ditch. Composure will be long in the coming. When the car finally nears the British army checkpoint half a mile from the Free State border, his mood sinks further. What's the hold up this time?

Some of the cars further along are doing a U-turn. He flags down one of the drivers.

'What's going on? Are they not letting the cars through?'

'From the looks of things they're checking every car going in and out of the Free State. Arms smuggling – supposedly there's been a tip off.'

'Thanks,' Paddy calls out as the driver moves off.

'I was going to drive out to Castlefin but we'll be here till dawn at this rate. We'll head back and go for an ice cream.'

'I don't want an ice cream. Can't we just sit in the car?'

'Kieran, we have to have a serious talk.'

'There's no need for a serious talk about anything. What's the big deal? Okay, I sometimes hang out the Duffy brothers. So what? That's it. End of story.'

Paddy's eyes are stinging and his mouth is parched. He swings into a U-turn which forces Kieran to grab hold of the dashboard. With one foot tapping the clutch and the other pressing down on the accelerator he swerves into the first lay-by he sees and slams on the brakes. The engine dies.

'Yes, we do need to have a serious talk.'

Kieran sits up straighter.

'Look at me when I'm talking to you, Kieran.'

'Okay, okay,' he mutters.

'If you want to be treated like an adult then you need to start acting like one. I'm tired of standing up for you when I'm not convinced you're telling the truth. So this is your chance to come clean. Your only chance. I can't help you if you're being dishonest. We'll start with the jumper. What really happened?'

Kieran's hesitation says it all. His silence squeezes hard into Paddy's windpipe. In those seconds he closes his eyes and succumbs to the images of Kieran being bullied at St Columb's.

'I lied about the jumper, but not about anything else.'

Oxygen surges back into Paddy's lungs.

'Go on.'

'I mean, I was there with the crowd when the army patrol appeared. But I didn't throw any stones. I was the first to crawl under the wire. The rest of them followed me after a minute.'

'What were you doing there in the first place? It wasn't

just the Duffy boys who were gathered at the top of the lane.'

'I was heading for the pitch. The Duffys were passing when I came out the door and we walked the length of the shop together. I didn't know they were meeting up with the head of the town crowd.'

Paddy lets Kieran's words hang in the air. Then twisting his body so that he's facing Kieran, he waits for his son to look at him.

'Okay, let's say I believe you this time' – the words are slow and deliberate – 'what I can't figure out is what you have in common with those boys.'

Another pause.

'I know they're members of the Provisional IRA Youth Movement. I also know that since Bloody Sunday, hundreds of young boys and men have been recruited and that the Duffy boys are active in recruiting. Are they putting pressure on you to join? Are they threatening you? Is that why you spend so much time with them? Are you scared?'

'No, no. You sound just like Mammy now. No one's bullying me or intimidating me or putting pressure on me.'

Paddy flinches.

'Why are you both so anti the Duffys?' Kieran asks. 'Or the IRA, for that matter. We all saw what happened on Bloody Sunday. Thirteen people shot dead for nothing, for protesting against internment.' Kieran is frustrated, angry. 'Any fool can see the British army isn't here to protect the Catholics.'

'Son, listen to me—'

'I'm not in the IRA, for God's sake, and I don't intend to be either. How many times do I have to say it before you believe me? Just because I've a strong opinion doesn't mean I'm going to take up the gun. Am I not allowed to have a bloody opinion?'

'No one said you're not entitled to an opinion, Kieran, so don't exaggerate – and don't swear.'

'I didn't swear – and I'm not the one around here who's exaggerating.' He grabs the back of his head. 'Da, come on, you've heard the way she goes on.'

'Don't refer to your mother as *she* – it's disrespectful.'

'Oh for God's sake, I didn't mean anything.' His hands have clamped his knees. 'What am I supposed to do or say to convince you both that this is all a load of nonsense? Okay, I'll stop hanging out with the Duffys so much. Will that keep her happy?'

'Kieran! What have I just said?'

'Okay, okay, I'm sorry … will that keep *Mammy* happy?'

Despite his sense that the battle is over and the situation has been diffused, Paddy gets no pleasure from the tone of defeat in Kieran's words.

'It's been a nerve-racking few days. Try to understand your mother. You know what she's like – she's a worrier. We'll go home now and I'll take her out for a drink. She's not going to be too pleased that you lied to her face more than once about the pullover. The trust is broken, so you'll have to work at getting it back.'

'Yeah, I know.'

Kieran is in a trance now.

'But I'll get her to see the truth in all this. Then we can put it to bed for good.'

The rev of the engine camouflages the heavy sigh that's been long in the coming.

No bright skyline now. Darkness and a drizzle. Both

force him to drive slower than he would like. Alertness, fuelled by an urgency to get back on amicable terms with Mairead, has replaced his earlier lethargy.

The town centre is deserted but for the usual loiterers. Murphy's is lit up. It's as good a pub as any, especially when there's a bit of live music on. But no, Mairead refuses to go there. Those airs and graces. He'll take her to Mulligan's. Plenty of peace and quiet. More her style. And there's usually a grand fire in the hearth. All positives on this occasion.

Now all he needs is for her to lighten up a bit. Getting her out of the house has become a chore at the best of times. But he's optimistic that the seeds have already been sown after he put his foot down with Kieran. He needs a drink if he's to get through an arduous plea bargain, because no matter what, he has to convince her they've nothing to worry about.

Kieran jumps out of the car almost before it comes to a standstill.

'How's about ye, Kieran lad?'

Riordan Duffy has popped out of nowhere and is calling from a few yards up the street.

'Not so bad, Mr Duffy. And yourself?'

Riordan, breathless, is almost at the car.

'Ah sure I can't complain. Paddy, any chance of a lift into town?' he asks through the half-open passenger door.

Kieran is stalling. Paddy puts the key back in the ignition.

'Go ahead on in, son. No problem, Riordan. In you get.'

Kieran is still hovering when the front door opens. What the hell? Has she nothing better to do?

'What are you standing in the rain for, Kieran?' Mairead is staring the bit out. If she had half a friendly tone in her voice, Paddy would be telling her to get spruced up for a night out on the town. But with a hatchet-face like that he'll be saying nothing.

'I'll be back in ten minutes,' he calls out instead and heads back down in the direction of town.

The drizzle is making way for a downpour and his wipers are on the blink again.

'Sorry, Riordan, I need to pull over for a second to get my wipers going.'

Riordan clears his throat, followed by a meek cough.

'Don't mind me, Paddy.' Another feeble cough. 'Truth is, I don't need a lift into town. That was just an excuse to catch you on your own for five minutes.'

'What's wrong?' The engine jerks to a stop. 'What is it? Is it Kieran?'

'What is it you're asking me?'

'You know fine well what I'm asking you, Riordan. Is Kieran caught up in any IRA activities?'

'What makes you ask that question? Has Kieran said anything to you?'

'No, he hasn't. He's saying he's not involved.' Paddy keeps his eyes diverted. The blow will come softer that way. 'Look, Riordan, just spit it out. It's why you're sitting here, isn't it?'

'As a matter of fact, Paddy, it's not Kieran I need to talk to you about. It's your niece Geraldine.'

'What? What about her?'

Again that bloody miserable fake cough.

'I'm sorry, Paddy, but word has it that she'll have to take the punishment. The boys at the top are saying things are too serious now. They can't make exceptions. It would set a precedent.'

'What are you talking about — *set a precedent*? Have you

seen the state of her? She watched her baby die for Christ sake!'

'I know, I know. I don't agree with the decision. I'm as sympathetic as the next man but—'

'Don't give me any bloody buts, Riordan. What kind of monsters are we becoming in this country? Tarring and feathering … it's barbaric!'

'Look, Paddy, it's got nothing to do with me. I'm just the messenger and not an official one at that. I'm sorry.'

'Is there nothing can be said or done? Is that it? You know a few people. Can you not do something? I'll owe you. You can't let them do it, Riordan.' Paddy's voice is barely a whisper.

Riordan opens the car door and pauses, staring at the dashboard.

'Actually, there's one man I can talk to but it's a long shot. Beyond that, there's nothing I can do.'

Paddy doesn't need to say a word for Riordan to feel the gratitude.

The rain has lightened up. He starts up the engine again and heads towards the main road into town where he picks up a bottle of Bushmills and six Babycham. A swig or two en route will go unnoticed.

Back at the house Sinead is getting the wee ones ready for bed. Mairead is in the kitchen. He goes in and pours himself a glass of water.

'Where did you go? I saw Riordan Duffy go back up the street fifteen minutes ago. And what was he doing in the car to begin with?'

'He wanted to give me a heads-up on the IRA's decision to punish Geraldine after all.'

'What?'

'You heard me right – a tarring and feathering.'

'Jesus, Paddy, is there nothing you can do?'

'It's not looking good. Riordan's on our side but his hands are tied.'

'But she's been home for over a month. She's only starting to come round. They can't be that callous. They won't go through with it.'

'They will go through with it. That's the way it is. Now we have to go over to Eileen and break the news. There's a very small chance Geraldine'll be saved, but we need to prepare Eileen for the worst. I've bought some Bushmills and Babycham to ease the blow.'

Mairead has picked up her coat and is moving towards the door. She's certainly calmed down from earlier on. He hangs back for a minute.

'Sinead, we're going over to Aunty Eileen's for a bit.'

He goes to the car where he'd left the drinks and twists the bag tight around the whiskey bottle.

'Here, grab that bag,' he says, handing Mairead the six pack of Babycham.

He's almost sure she isn't going to bring up the subject of Kieran when lo and behold she opens her mouth to speak. Jesus Christ! Does she never get tired of it?

'Did you get anywhere with Kieran? I'm just asking.'

At least she's showing a bit of diplomacy. Yes, it's an ill-timed question. Selfish even. But he's no need to take the gloves off. Her voice is soft. Perhaps she's getting tired of it all too. At last.

'Kieran's not involved with the IRA in any shape or form, Mairead.'

They are walking in unison.

'Did Riordan tell you that?'

'Yes … and our son told me too.'

They are on Eileen's doorstep. He positions his fingertip on the door bell, pausing for a second to face her.

'I'm telling you, Mairead, categorically, without a shadow of a doubt, Kieran is not caught up in this madness or ever will be. Now can we let it go? Please?'

The shrill of the doorbell nearly drowns Mairead's reply.

But Paddy's hearing is sharp. His ears never deceive him.

'Yes, Paddy.'

He breathes out and leads the way into Eileen's front room.

1978

Epilogue

THE CASKET IS CLOSED. No serene face to suspend reality for the mourners at this particular wake. There is no face at all – only pieces of what might have been Kieran Reilly's body. They were found amidst the rubble of Danny Lynch's scullery where the incendiary device they were making had prematurely exploded. An official statement has not been released but it is believed that both men were active members of the Provisional Irish Republican Army.

Unfortunately, at a wake like this one the usual condolences and cups of tea are tainted. Two men are dead. A tragedy. But the incendiary device they were making may have killed many more had it reached its true destination. There is no reconciling these polarised truths. So for now, the mourners try to do what they are there for: provide support for a family that is grieving. Satisfying curiosity, making judgements, rationalising what happened, appeasing consciences – these needs are tucked away for the time being.

But eventually they will resurface.

The mother of the deceased will be the first to face the people's jury. Did she not know her eldest son was a member of the IRA? Is it possible that she was so naive? She's in shock. She says her son was not involved. She appears to be telling the truth. Her truth. She is to be pitied.

Mairead Reilly is sitting in her living room, a moist handkerchief in one hand and a cigarette in the other. She is a woman with gaunt features and lifeless eyes that once had a potential for beauty. Seven births and a husband she now detests will keep her this way for a long, long time. Shame and grief battle for supremacy. Shame will win. Mairead Reilly does not cope well with public scrutiny. She is a proud woman, like her mother. People's opinions matter. So her shame and pride will eat at her soul; it will consume her, devour her piece by piece, swallow her up. But she will be oblivious to this inner process. Mairead Reilly will get on with life in the dutiful, stoic manner of her ancestors.

But what about the father, Patrick Reilly? What do the townspeople have to say about him? Surely he must have known? Wasn't he a friend and confidante of Danny Lynch? The liaison probably goes way back. Aren't they both teachers? A coincidence? Word has it that Paddy Reilly refused to let his son attend St Columb's boarding school. What was that about? Was Kieran Reilly even offered a scholarship? Maybe not. But certainly his poor mother wanted nothing more than for her son to get the best education in the county. He'd probably be at university now like his sister. What would Kieran Reilly know about bomb-making? What business did he have being down in Danny Lynch's house? That's a pertinent question the townspeople would very much like an answer to. Among others. Like why

Geraldine Donnelly did not get tarred and feathered for her crime. Perhaps because some girls are fortunate enough to have people in high places?

Paddy Reilly, who is standing at a distance from his family, will also battle with intense shame. But unlike his wife, he cares little about idle gossip and takes no responsibility for the machinations of small-town imaginations. His shame is fuelled by demons that are nesting in his soul. Faced with this new trauma in his life, his brand of shame will lead him further down the neck of a whiskey bottle. Or a vodka bottle. In fact, any bottle that can dispel the stink emanating from his darkest secrets. He will continue to believe in values like honesty, peace and integrity while sinking further into his own weaknesses, his humanness, a paradox that will confuse and eventually disappoint a few of his children, especially his eldest daughter, Sinead.

Where the Reilly children are concerned, the townspeople gathered in the wake house will feel compassion and a generous dose of pity. There will be allowances made when future misdemeanours occur. Kieran Reilly's siblings are not to blame for anything.

The younger children are not present at the wake. They are staying with a neighbour. But Sinead, Niamh and Niall are standing close to their mother. Absence of emotion can be a natural reaction to shock. It's a common fact. Their tears will come in time. Hopefully. For their sake. But then again, the tears may never come. The Reilly clan has an inordinate propensity for quashing emotion. It is learned behaviour, a survival mechanism carried down through both sets of genes. A quick glance across the room provides living proof of this.

For those who know her story, the children's

grandmother is enough to remind them of how resilient a human being can be when faced with tragedy and injustice. No one in the town has witnessed a tear from Margaret Boyle. And no one is ever likely to. Not now. Not since the early onset of dementia has given her a safe haven in which to spend the rest of her days. She is content. She has become accustomed to the bedlam of the Reilly household and sharing a bedroom with Niamh and Shauna, though she's finding it difficult to grasp what has been going on these last few nights. It has something to do with Sinead being home on holiday. Margaret Boyle will be pleased when Sinead goes back to university.

Sinead is standing with her brother and sister near the front window of their living room. She too will be pleased when she goes back to university. Her gaze scans the snow spread evenly over the Green. By tomorrow evening there will be no wake house overshadowing the excitement of the youngsters playing outside. More snowmen will have sprouted. It's unfortunate that Sinead was born with a vivid imagination. Her brain had morphed into a kaleidoscope of horrors after the news of Kieran's death. Images of dismembered limbs and burning flesh had stayed with her on the plane across the Irish Sea, into the Arrivals lounge at Aldergrove Airport and in the car where she had endured an agonising two-hour journey sitting next to her father in silence. It was only on entering 7 Drummore Court that the images had ceased to torment her.

Now, on the second day of the wake, she is in control. There is no reason why she should have to stay for more than a couple of days after the funeral. Niamh will have to step up to the mark. Sinead has a new life now. She's not like her mother. She will do things differently. Her children will have happy parents. In England, she has a clean slate. No past. No Mass. No confession. Anonymity. She will leave the old Sinead Riley behind on Irish soil. That persona has no place in her life now.

She snaps out of her reverie and dutifully goes into the kitchen. Serving tea and biscuits will keep her distracted and kill time. This flutter of faith in a fairy-tale future has lightened her step, slowed her breathing, eased the nausea. In a few days, she'll be running across the Arrivals lounge at Heathrow to where her friend will be waiting for her.

And this brand new Sinead Reilly plans to keep running.

But what she is unaware of, and blissfully so, is that no matter how fast she learns to run, it will never be fast enough.

Acknowledgements

Thanks to:

Averill Buchanan, my editor, for her advice and guidance; Sarah Corbett, my tutor at Lancaster University, and my fellow aspiring writers on the course, especially Liz, Olivia and Ericka; my cousin Dolores for giving me permission to use the photograph on the cover; my friends, especially Maria and Kostas; my mother and father; all my brothers and sisters, especially Brid and Dermot who read story after story and believed in the book even when I didn't; my niece Amanda for always being there; and my daughters Helena and Melina for their unconditional love and support.

ABOUT THE AUTHOR

DEIRDRE FOLEY was born in County Tyrone, Northern Ireland. She studied and worked in London as a welfare officer before moving to Athens, where she lived for many years teaching English and bringing up her two daughters. Now she is a writer and a gestalt psychotherapist. She has an MA in Creative Writing from Lancaster University, and in 2014 she was shortlisted for the Fish Short Memoir Competition. She flits between her two homelands, Ireland and Greece, and is working on a second novel.